The Hookup Artist

Also by Tucker Shaw

NONFICTION

Dreams (2000)

Any Advice? (2000)

This Book Is About Sex (2000)

Who Do You Think You Are? (2001)

Peace (2002)

What's That Smell? Oh, It's Me. (2003)

FICTION

Flavor of the Week (2003)

Confessions of a Backup Dancer (2004)

The Hookup Artist

Tucker Shaw

HarperCollins*Publishers*

Produced by Alloy Entertainment
151 West 26th Street, New York, NY 10001

Library of Congress Cataloging-in-Publication Data available.

1 2 3 4 5 6 7 8 9 10
◆
First Edition

For Jenn.
I'm appalled.

Acknowledgments

Many, many thanks to Dan Mandel for the continued sound advice.

Thanks to Alloy Entertainment for all the hard work—Ben, Josh, Les, Judy, Lynn, everyone. You're the best! Thanks to the entire HarperCollins crew. And great big ups to Pam for putting it all in perspective.

1.

Thursday

"*AY*, LUCAS, I DON'T CARE *HOW* GAY YOU ARE," SAID SONJA AS I tried to keep my hands on her swiveling hips. "White boys just can't dance." She pushed my shoulders away in frustration and retied her apron.

"You would know, Sonja," I answered, still swaying to the old Selena song that was blaring from La Boca's shabby old jukebox. "After all, you've *danced* with every white guy at school. Not to mention every Mexican guy, every black guy, every student teacher . . ."

Sonja snapped her towel at me as I flipped another red vinyl chair up onto table four, which she'd just wiped down. "Well, if I could find one who knows how to dance, maybe . . ."

"Shut up, you two," barked Cate. She looked up from the stack of dinner checks she was tallying in booth one and tucked a dirty-blond lock behind her ear. "You're making me lose count." She readjusted her leg, which she'd propped up on a chair pulled in next to the booth. "Ouch," she said.

"Pass-around Patty over here is the only one who's losing count," I said, pointing at Sonja, who'd just then bent over to retrieve a spoon from under table eleven. "Are you ever *not* thinking about guys?"

"You should talk, Mr. Totally Obsessed With His New Boyfriend," said Sonja, standing back up and snapping her gum. "What's his name? Marco? Marcus? Marty? The one who plays the piano or whatever?" She flipped her hair—no small feat, considering the pile of rich, weighty curls that fell halfway down her back and looked, well, *heavy*—and spun toward table thirteen, wiggling her butt to the beat and brushing tortilla crumbs into her hand. *"Bidi-bidi bom-bom . . ."* she sang, her voice filling the empty dining room. Sonja practically grew up at La Boca Mexicana, her father's small, gaudy, sixteen-table strip-mall cantina on Hampden Avenue. And ever since Sonja learned how to control the jukebox, Selena was a constant presence. "Martin! Is it Martin? *Bidi-bidi bom-bom . . ."*

"Marcus," I said, knowing she wasn't listening anyway. "His name is Marcus. And he plays the guitar." *Beautifully,* I added to myself. "Marcus." I savored the way my mouth moved around the word. *Marcus.* It felt like ice cream, and I didn't want to share, not yet. I wanted Marcus all to myself, forever.

Stop! I didn't want to jinx it. I didn't want to hope. Last time I'd hoped too much, with Tim, the whole thing blew up in my face. He'd laughed when I told him how I felt. I couldn't believe that in all my years of matchmaking, it had taken me until then to realize: The trick was *not* to hope. Not for myself, anyway. I'd save my hope for the people I set up.

"Can you please turn that down?" shouted Cate, clipping together a handful of receipts. "I can't concentrate!"

"You know, Cate," I said, "when you're not so grouchy, you're one of the prettiest girls I know!" It was true. Her eyes were clear and big and green, and her hair, when she let it down, moved like silk. Guys liked Cate, but many stayed away. She had a high-minded air about her, an intelligence, an aloofness. With the right makeup and a thong, she had the raw material to be a *Maxim* girl. But Cate didn't think much of *Maxim* girls.

Sonja stopped dancing and walked, stiffly, over to the jukebox in the corner. She reached behind where the employees-only volume controls were and, instead of turning it down, turned it up. *Way* up. "*Bidi-bidi bom-bom!*" she belted, taunting Cate. Cate grabbed a spoon and tossed it at Sonja, who blocked it with her hip, sending it clanging to the floor. "I will never turn down Selena," she said with a sniff. "*La reina.* In San Antonio she's considered a goddess! She is the angel of Corpus Christi!"

"Sonja," I said gently, "Selena is dead. You know that, right?" I put my hand on the back of her shoulder. "The queen of south Texas has been dead for ten years."

"Lucas!" gasped Cate. "You mentioned the unmentionable!"

"And you live," I added, "in Denver. Not Corpus Christi."

Sonja's shoulder stiffened under my fingers, and she inhaled sharply.

"You were in second grade when she died," I continued. "One day you'll make that pilgrimage to Corpus Christi to worship at her altar, but in the meantime, she would want you to expand your horizons."

"*No me toca,*" said Sonja, wrenching her shoulder away from my hand. She walked over to the jukebox and turned it up still higher. "*La reina,*" she growled.

I smiled. I was happy. It was the precious end of another Thursday-night dinner shift, and I was with my girls. My stubborn girls. We were fighting, but not really, because we were together. And it was still summer and Selena was the queen.

Later, things would only get better, when I would see Marcus again, for the first time since . . . I looked at my watch. For the first time since three thirty this afternoon, after he'd serenaded me with some song by the White Stripes and we'd had our second hands-on make-out session of the day. I'd left him at his place, snoozing, beautiful, unworried, with a note stuck between the strings of his guitar. It was a request: WRITE A SONG FOR ME.

I imagined him there still, dreaming next to my note, under an invisible cloud of his sweet, sweet breath, waiting for me, perfect.

Okay, gross. If I was listening to myself talk like this, I'd tell myself to snap out of it. I flipped another chair onto table four, surprised at how light it felt. Everything felt lighter tonight.

The song finally came to an end and the room went quiet, revealing a ruckus on the other side of the swinging kitchen door. Pots and pans bashing, dishes crashing against each other, and competing voices, one deep and rich, one tinny and stressed, singing over a Mexican pop song, both *way* off-key.

Sonja scoffed, smiling. "My musical family," she muttered, then yelled, "Dad! El Jefe! You guys! Keep it down." She walked over to the jukebox to cue up another Selena tune. "So, Lucas," she said. "When are you finally going to set me up with Mike Maccabee, anyway? That guy from the football team?"

Mike Maccabee—one of Thomas Jefferson's least talented defensive linemen and all-around meathead—was the current object of Sonja's swiftly shifting affections. I'd set Tabitha Zimmerman up with him last year. It had been so easy. One day when they were passing each other in the hallway, I whipped out my digital camera. All it took was a simple, "Hey, you two, stand a little closer and smile!" to get them to put their arms around each other. Then I'd e-mailed both of them the picture at the same time. Mike and Tabitha saw how good they looked together, and they already had each other's e-mail addresses. And so the rest was history. That is, until he puked on her during a drunken make-out session. The vomit seemed to extinguish that spark.

"Sonja, gross. But you don't need my help with him anyway. Just wear a tank top."

"Very funny," she said, hiking up her jeans.

"You don't have time for Maccabee anyway," I pointed

out. "I believe I've got you down for coffee with Brandon tonight after work. Then Desi tomorrow afternoon for a 'study session,' or is it the other way around? And I know there's someone on the schedule for the day after that. You're booked, sweetie."

"But Mike's hot," whined Sonja. "There's always time for hot. Come on!"

"Mike Maccabee is hot; this is true. But Mike Maccabee is an idiot," I said. "Big, dumb, and horny." I flipped another chair.

"Perfect," said Sonja. "Just my type. So come on, matchmaker." She threw a handful of crumpled green napkins at me. "Hook me up!"

"Too easy," I said. "Give me a *challenge*! How about Eric Davenport? They say he's the next Tiger Woods."

"*Ay*, Lucas," said Sonja. "Have you seen what he has to wear on the course? The guy is covered in pleats."

"You're so deep, Sonja," I said. "So willing to look below the surface. I admire that, how you never judge a book by its cover."

"*Pleats,*" said Sonja gravely. "And a braided belt."

"Point taken," I conceded. "David Rangel? The shortstop?" I said absentmindedly, flipping another chair. With Sonja, it was a matter of running through the list until you found someone she liked but also hadn't dated yet. It wasn't easy. "Adam Pettijean? He was all-state in cross-country."

"Lucas, you set me up with him last year. Remember? St. Patrick's Day? When you ditched me at O'Keegan's party?"

"I did not *ditch* you," I said. "I simply got in the car and took off, leaving you without a ride home. I knew Adam would offer to drive you when I asked him to tell you I'd had to leave and he should tell you good-bye for me. Whatever happened with him, anyway?"

"I forget," said Sonja. "But I already dated him, so what difference does it make?"

"It might be time to do some recycling, Sonja," I said. "It's not like cute hot single guys are an unlimited resource, you know. We're running out of candidates!"

"Come on, Lucas. Mike!"

"What about Alex Norita?" blurted Cate, out of nowhere. "You know, from our trig class last year? Well, from Lucas's and my trig class. Didn't you see when he came in tonight to pick up a take-home tub of chili con queso? I think he's the sweetest kid. And I know he likes you, Sonja. Didn't you see him staring at you?"

I was pretty shocked. *Alex Norita?* Cate nodded, and I decided to play along. "It's true," I said to Sonja. "He was staring."

"Excuse me?" scoffed Sonja, lips pursed. "Have you two completely lost it? Last time I saw Alex Norita, he was in a black turtleneck, camped out at the mall three days before the release of the new *Star Trek* movie. The guy thinks Klingers are real."

"Klingons," I said. "Maybe you should call him!"

Sonja cocked her head back and wagged her finger in the air. "Don't be gross, Lucas. I outweigh the kid by thirty pounds. But why don't you set *Cate* up with Alex if she thinks he's so sweet?"

"Sonja," said Cate, "you know I've sworn off boys. *Forever.*"

I turned over one last chair, then collapsed in the booth next to Cate. "Yeah, Sonja," I said. "Leave Cate alone. It's only been four short weeks since she busted Vince tonsil-deep in Christy Canyons, I mean Christy Campbell." I sucked in my breath sharply and rested my hand on Cate's arm. "Just two days after Cate's debilitating knee surgery." *Marcus would never do that to me.*

"Shut up," said Cate, pulling her arm back. "It wasn't that major, just a tendon thing. The injury was minor. My knee is going to be fine. I've been walking on it fine."

"I still want to take down that bitch who pushed you in the fourth quarter," said Sonja. "She cost you guys the championship."

"Sonja," I said, "quit acting like you know anything about sports."

"*¡Ya no, ya no!*" sang Sonja.

"That was a horror show," said Cate. "And I hate horror shows."

"Me too!" yelled Sonja. "I refuse to go to horror movies ever since I saw that first *Revenge of the Dead* movie. They freak me out." She shuddered and stuck out her tongue. "What are they on now, like, *Revenge of the Dead, Part Twenty-Two?*"

"Cate, that's it," I said, taking her hand. "Promise you'll let *us* pick your next boyfriend, okay? I mean, you're good at soccer. You're good at school. You're good at adding up receipts. But you suck at picking boys. You *always* pick jerks."

"Yeah, but jerks are hot," said Sonja, swaying past the jukebox. "You know what I mean? The biggest jerks are always the hottest guys."

"Listen to yourself, Sonja." I shook my head at Cate. "Honestly."

Cate snapped her hand away from my grasp. "No boys." She tucked her hair behind her ear and went back to her receipts.

I turned to Sonja, who'd just reached into her apron, where her cell phone was chirping Selena's "*No Me Queda Mas.*" "Hello?" she said. "Who is this?"

I selected the best corn chip from the basket sitting there and dragged it through a bowl of the warm, cheesy, peppery, jalapeño-laced chili con queso, La Boca's best and most famous dish. It had won Best Appetizer in *Denver* magazine's annual "Best of Denver" list four years in a row, and now every table ordered it. There was no secret as to why— it was freaking delicious. El Jefe, Sonja's stout, balding father, with his long scraggly ponytail and blue bandanna headband, was proud of his CCQ.

"What?" I heard Sonja saying. "But we have plans!"

Opening my mouth as wide as I could, I carefully placed the warm, CCQ-coated chip on my tongue. I closed my lips around it, mashing it on the roof of my mouth, shattering the chip and spreading the smoky, creamy, spicy cheese across my tongue.

"Whatever," moped Sonja into her phone.

I wondered if Marcus would love it as much as I did. I imagined us ten years from now, visiting Denver from New York, where we'd live in a fabulous loft with two Portuguese water dogs and a recording studio for Marcus. We'd stop by La Boca, and El Jefe, still at the stove beneath the picture of Jesus, would make us a fresh batch of CCQ because he could see how in love we still were. Sigh. *Gag.*

"Yum," I said to the air. "Love that stuff." I dipped another chip, humming along to Selena. *"Amor prohibido . . ."*

"Ugh. Do you even know what that means?" asked Sonja, sliding into the booth next to me and checking her hair in one of the multitude of mosaic-framed antique (or antique-*like*) mirrors that covered the walls of the small restaurant. "Hm?"

"'Forbidden love,'" I said, tugging at the string of chili-pepper-shaped decorative lights that hung on the wall. "Don't forget, I took Spanish in ninth grade."

"Ay, Lucas, *please,"* said Sonja. "I hate boys."

"Did you just get blown off?" I asked.

"Second time this weekend," she said. "I hate him."

"Which one was it?" I asked. "Brandon or Desi?"

"Brandon," said Sonja. "He's probably going back with Jenny Mansfield, aka Miss Skinny-ass Barbie Doll, who's been saving for her boob job since she was fifteen. I hate him. I hate high school boys."

She scooped herself a chip full of CCQ and crunched it slowly. "Mmm." And then another. And another. Her head hung and her movements slowed as she allowed her disappointment to wallow its way into the gooey, warm bowl of CCQ.

Selena wrapped up *"Amor Prohibido"* with her typical, no-question-about-it finality and the room went silent for a moment. But only for a moment, as the first synth-violin strains of *"Fotos y Recuerdos"* revved up. Sonja dropped her chip and leaped up from the booth, her heartbreak miraculously, instantly healed. "I love this song!"

"Really?" asked Cate, giggling. "You love a Selena song? Lucas, can you believe it?"

"That's our girl," I said.

Sonja grabbed my forearm and dragged me up and out of the booth. She grabbed me by the waist and started moving our hips together, back and forth, in little circles, tapping my waist to follow hers, grinding. "This is called the washing machine. I saw it in *Selena*. See, hip to hip, move in little circles. Watch my ass, see?" Sonja slapped herself on the butt. "Brandon just couldn't handle *this*."

I groaned, but she kept grinding. "The washing machine. You can teach that to Marcus later. You *are* seeing him later, aren't you? You *do* like this one, don't you? *Amor prohibido . . .*"

"Shhh," I said, pushing her away, thinking, *Don't jinx it.* I wasn't ready to talk about Marcus. It wasn't time to talk, not yet. Marcus and I had only been together for a few days. There would be plenty of time to talk about it. And when I finally did tell the girls just how big this was, how everything was finally happening for me, they'd be happy. So there was no rush. Marcus and I were free—free to take our time, free to fall in love, perfectly.

Not that word again, I reminded myself. Still, my stomach flushed, warm.

"Someone's in love," said Cate sarcastically. "Lucas and Marcus sitting in a tree . . . Look, Sonja! He's blushing!"

She was right: I was blushing. I could feel it. "Shut up!" I laughed, grabbing a tub of dirty dishes and crashing through the employees-only swinging door into the kitchen, which was spacious but crowded with equipment and dishes. El Jefe was watching two of Sonja's older brothers, Tony and Gabriel, wrestle with the industrial dishwasher. Gabriel, impatient, was trying to squeeze another rack of water glasses into it.

"It won't fit!" shouted Tony, just as Gabriel gave the rack one last wobbly shove and let go. Tony dove but was too late—the rack crashed to the ground, glass shattering everywhere. The room went silent for a split second. Tony began shouting in a kind of Spanish that we never learned in ninth grade. "*¡Pendejo! ¿Qué haces?*"

"*¡Dios mío!*" shouted El Jefe, clipping Tony's tirade. His voice was booming, low, and liquid, and it commanded our attention. I followed El Jefe's gaze up over the big industrial stove to the right of the exhaust hood, where three pictures hung. One was a photo of El Jefe with all five of his kids, taken two years ago. One was Jesus—a bloody, dramatic, scraggly, thrift-store, Technicolor Jesus—his body slumped on the cross, his face grimacing, eyes cast up in exhaustion.

Between these two pictures was a photo of Sonja's mother, a beautiful woman with thick, dark hair and wide-set doe eyes. She wore a 1980s-era pink shaker-knit sweater, shoulder pads and all, and she was smiling broadly, a gummy grin that was just like Sonja's. She'd died of cervical cancer just seven months after Sonja was born.

El Jefe closed his eyes, crossed himself, and returned to the walk-in freezer. Tony, silent now, tapped Gabriel on the shoulder and pointed at the broken glass. Gabriel nodded and went to get a broom.

I grabbed a La Boca matchbook off the shelf to my left and quickly scribbled.

Cate slipped through the swinging door, limping slightly. "I can't take any more Selena," she said, dropping a bucket of silverware on the counter. She spun back around and exited, catching the still-swinging door as it opened into the dining room. "Get out here," she said. "It's tip time."

I followed her out into the dining room, where Sonja was fishing through her apron pockets. "Cough it up."

I handed Sonja my pathetic wad of crumpled singles and two fistfuls of coins. "Oh," I said, smiling. "And this is for you." I handed her the matchbook. "Now that you're free later."

Sonja snatched the matchbook out of my hand, opening it up. "'4 a good time, call Alex Norita,'" she read aloud. "'555-4224'? Are you kidding me?" She threw it at me wildly, but I reached quickly and snatched it out of the air, feeling clever.

"I gotta pee," I said, winking at Cate. "Be right back."

I sauntered back to the hall where the phone and bathrooms

were, one labeled MUJERES and one labeled HOMBRES. For kicks, I chose MUJERES.

I locked the door behind me and unzipped. There was a full-length mirror right inside. I thought I looked pretty good. I needed a haircut, maybe, and I guess I'd rather be six feet tall instead of five foot nine, but I was in pretty good shape. Straight teeth, flat stomach, nice shoulders. Not bad.

I wondered if Marcus thought so.

Marcus. Marcus, who looked perfect to me. Floppy brown hair, an eyebrow ring, hazy blue eyes, dirty jeans, flip-flops, and incredible lips. I couldn't get over his lips. From the first time I saw them, singing along to a Ben Jelen track at the Sound Warehouse. They were full, his lips, red and alive. I wanted to look more like him.

Last night, we'd driven Marcus's pickup out to Chatfield Dam to, as he described it, watch the stars. I watched his lips while he told me about Elliott, his ex, the older guy who'd dumped him, then taken him back, then dumped him again. Marcus scratched his head. He said he didn't care. He said he was glad Elliott was gone, because it opened the door for me.

Last night was the first time Marcus sang to me. An old Don McLean song called "Starry Starry Night" or something.

"This world was never meant for one as beautiful as you," he sang. I laid my head in his lap while his soothing voice dripped over me, and decided that I'd never be happier than this. I swore to myself that someday I'd make Marcus

know that I'd never leave him like Elliott. What Elliott had broken, I'd fix.

We made out on the dam for hours that night and, later, in the car.

I was afraid, sort of, but he never let go of me. More experienced than I was, Marcus made me feel safe. He was like a seat belt, an air bag, a security blanket. I knew I was all right with Marcus; I never closed my eyes. I felt grown-up with him, mature. This was way beyond high school love. This was the real thing: honest, open, complete.

For so long I'd just assumed I was cursed, that I'd always be a matchmaker but never make a match for myself. I mean, cliché, right? But I just figured that was my life story. Besides, last I checked, a guy can't marry another guy anyway. So why bother fantasizing about it?

But Marcus made me think differently. He made it seem possible.

"*No!*" I snapped at myself aloud. *Don't say that. Don't even think it.* I flushed and rinsed off my hands.

I unlatched the MUJERES door, opening it right into Sonja, who was standing in front of the full-length mirror opposite the door, hiking up her shirt to reveal her belly button. El Jefe appeared at the kitchen door just then and hissed. He motioned at Sonja to pull down her shirt, shaking his head disapprovingly.

Sonja pulled down her shirt, deflated. "He is so out of it." She handed me some bills. "Here, thirty-two dollars."

"That's it? For six hours?"

"Welcome to America," said Sonja. "Land of Plenty."

"I think this is yours," I said, handing Alex Norita's matchbook back to her. "Maybe Cate's onto something. You'd never do math homework again."

"*Callate*," muttered Sonja. We both looked over at Cate, who was locking the front door and shouting through the glass at a figure I couldn't see, "Sorry! We're closed!" She drew her finger across her neck. "Closed!" She turned back to us, green eyes rolling.

"Who is that?" yelled El Jefe from the kitchen.

"No one," Sonja yelled back. Then she turned to Cate. "Who is it? Is he cute? Is it Mike Maccabee?"

"Down, girl," I said to Sonja. "*¡Cerrado!*" I shouted at the door.

But the figure wasn't leaving, and there was another knock. The three of us looked at one another. "Stand back, ladies," I said. "Allow me." I unlocked the door just a crack and said without looking up, "The kitchen is closed. Sorry." I had begun pushing the door closed when a hand thrust out, blocking it open.

"Hey, Lucas." That voice.

I looked up to see Marcus, perfect Marcus, eyebrow ring, hazy eyes, and all. Instantly everything in me lifted—my chin, my shoulders, my hands, my toes! Marcus was here!

"Marcus," I said dumbly, trying to keep upright. "You're here." I was buzzing from somewhere below my stomach, flushed with warmth and lust and anxiety and worry. Had he written my song?

Marcus had surprised me at work! I was being surprised at work by my *boyfriend*.

I stepped forward to kiss him, arms rising slowly for his shoulders, aiming for his lips, anticipating the perfect fit they'd make with mine. Just like last night.

But Marcus pulled back, cold. "No, Lucas," he said. He pushed his hair away from his face, and then it instantly fell back into his eyes.

"Oh, it's okay," I said, motioning to Cate and Sonja. "They're cool. They know about me."

Marcus nodded at the girls. "Hi," he said. Then, turning back to me and casting his eyes at my feet, "That's not what I mean. Can I talk to you for a second?"

"Sure!" I tried to sound normal, but I was feeling shaky. "What's up?" Why wasn't he looking at me?

"I mean alone," he said quietly. "There's something I have to talk to you about."

No, I thought. *He didn't just say that.* "Okay," I said, mind racing, foggy. What did this mean? *There's something I have to talk to you about.* What did he have to tell me? Was it bad?

I turned and looked at Sonja, who pushed past me, aggressive, holding out one hand to Marcus. "I'm Sonja," she said. "And you are?" She threw her other arm in front of me, like a driver protecting her passenger when she stops too short.

"Sonja," said Cate urgently, reaching around me to take her arm. "I think we have some things to take care of in the kitchen. Those salt shakers need refilling."

Sonja stood firm, still staring at Marcus, beautiful Marcus.

"It's okay," I whispered to Sonja while I searched Marcus's eyes. "Leave us alone. I'll get you later."

Sonja backed up slowly, still glaring at Marcus. Cate took her by the elbow and backed her into the kitchen.

I held the door open for Marcus, smiling weakly, trying not to betray the deepening pit in my gut. Maybe this wasn't bad news. "Don't mind Sonja," I choked, motioning for him to come in. "Come on in. We can have some flan." I tried to duck down into his line of vision, hoping to break his stare from his shoes. *Look at me!*

"No, that's okay," he said, tugging at his eyebrow ring. "I can't come in."

I noticed that his truck was still running and the headlights were on.

"Listen," said Marcus. "Last night was really fun, but . . ."

Suddenly I couldn't hear anything but the back of my throat as I swallowed hard, a dry, drawn-out swallow of fear and desperation. "But?" I managed. "But what?"

"Lucas, I wanted to tell you—I didn't expect anything to come of this. Elliott found your note this afternoon, and he made me come here tonight to tell you I can never see you again." Marcus held up the note, eyes still cast down. "He's in the truck."

I stood, blank, immobile, confused. I wasn't sure what was happening. Was I being dumped? Was I being tested? Maybe this didn't matter. Maybe Marcus was going to tell me that he just needed some time to get rid of his boyfriend. He really loved *me*!

"Marcus," I said. "I . . ." *Look at me!*

"I have to go," he said. He stuffed the note into my front pocket. "This is yours."

"Marcus?"

"Good-bye, Lucas," he said, without turning around. "Have a good one."

I stared at him for a moment and tried to find the words to respond. "Okay," was all I could come up with. Marcus turned and broke into a trot. He climbed into the passenger seat of the truck, and the truck sped away. I never did get a look at the driver.

I stood for a moment, staring after the truck's taillights as they slipped onto Hampden Avenue and melted into the always-heavy traffic. What was I supposed to do now? I didn't understand. I couldn't.

I turned, slowly, back into the dining room and looked for something, *anything,* to do.

"I'll kill him!" screamed Sonja, blasting her way through the dining room. She threw herself out the door and into the strip-mall parking lot. "Where'd he go?!"

"I don't know. I think he's gone," I said. "I don't know."

"Lucas," said Cate, taking my arm. "Lucas."

"Were you guys listening at the door?" I said. "That's so uncool."

"Duh," said Cate, pacing with me, holding on. "Of course we were listening at the door. We're your girls."

She was right. Duh. I would have been listening too.

"Lucas." She was still talking. "I know what you're feeling."

I hate when people say that. She had no idea. "Do you?" I challenged, narrowing my eyes. "Do you really?"

"News flash! I just got dumped too. Remember?" She kept pacing. "Can we stop for a second? My knee . . ."

I stopped. She didn't understand. Straight people can't. Everything is different for them. But she *wanted* to understand, and that was all I was gonna get.

"I'm fine," I said, breathless. "I'm totally fine."

"I know," she said, taking hold of the back of my head. "You're my Lucas. Of course you're fine." She reached up to stroke my hair. "You'll get through this."

"I don't know," I said. "This time, I don't know."

I didn't cry for a couple of minutes, but once I started, it lasted a while. Cate held on to me the whole time, but I still felt lonely.

2.

Thursday

"YOU'RE WHAT?" GASPED SONJA. SHE PUSHED HER SUNGLASSES up onto her forehead and checked her lip liner in her compact mirror *again*.

"You heard me," I repeated from behind my own faux-tortoiseshell wraparounds. "I'm done with boys. Finished. My store *está cerrado*. I no longer care about that crap. It's official. As of today, the day of the Thomas Jefferson Schedule Fair, I proclaim myself boy-free."

Cate patted my shoulder. "I'm with you," she said. "No more boys." She ruffled the stack of papers in her hand.

"*Ay*, you two," said Sonja, looking at her nails.

"Not *you*, Cate," I said. "Just me. No more boys for me."

"No, for me too. It's hopeless. Every boy I date turns out to be a dick."

"Like Vince?" asked Sonja, smoothing down her skirt. "Is this too short?" she asked.

"Yes," answered Cate. "I mean no. I mean, no about the skirt. Yes about Vince being a dick. What was I thinking? I *knew* he was a jerk. But he was so nice to me. And he's such a good soccer player."

"Lame!" I barked.

"Plus he's hot," said Sonja. "Have you seen his chest?"

"Lame!" I scoffed. I thought about Vince's often-displayed chest . . . smooth, muscular, tan. "Lame!"

"I know," whined Cate. "I don't know. I guess I just figured that since we had soccer in common, maybe he'd change. For me." Cate started walking across the parking lot toward the south side of the square, brick, personality-free, mammoth 1985-ish high-Reagan-era building, Thomas Jefferson High School. "That's what my instincts were telling me anyway."

As if on cue, Sonja followed, shaking her head. "I saw an episode of *Oprah* about this once: smart women who make stupid choices," she said. "You're not alone. It's, like, a scientific thing."

"I thought he would change," said Cate, banging her open palm against her head. "Stupid, stupid, stupid."

Sonja reached out to catch Cate's hand. "Don't beat yourself up over it." She threw one arm around Cate's shoulders. "You may be stupid about boys, but at least you're not stupid about *everything*. At least you're not Christy Canyons."

"Yeah, Cate," I said, still thinking about Vince's chest. "At least you're not Christy Canyons."

"Wowee," said Cate. "At least I'm not a slut."

"Seriously, though," I said. "Cate, ignore your instincts for now. Trust us instead."

"Yeah!" squealed Sonja. "That's a really good idea. In fact, let's make it an official thing! Promise you'll let Lucas pick your next boyfriend!"

"What next boyfriend?" said Cate.

"Just promise!"

"Will it shut you up?" asked Cate. "Fine. I promise that Lucas can set me up with my nonexistent next boyfriend. But since there will be no next boyfriend, this is a meaningless promise."

"Gee, thanks," I said.

"Back to you, Lucas." Sonja clucked, throwing her other arm around my shoulders. "I'm still not buying it. No more boys? You said the same thing after Tim back in July. Six weeks later, hello Marcus. School starts next Tuesday, so I see a new boyfriend for you by homecoming."

"Wrong," I said. "I'm twice bitten in two months. I refuse to be the jackass who gets dumped three times in a row."

And I meant it. Over the week since Marcus had dumped me, I'd decided something: All of this was just a matter of priorities. So if I took boys off my list of things I cared about, then I couldn't care about Marcus. And if I didn't care about Marcus, then everything was cool. So, I'd just not care about boys at all. Easy.

Okay, so maybe it didn't make *perfect* sense. But it was all I had to hang on to. I needed *something*.

"That's dumb," said Sonja. "But since *you* won't be

dating, you'll have more time to hook me up with Maccabee! In fact, there he is! Hey, Mike!" Sonja jumped up and waved across the parking lot at the group of football players standing around looking at Mike Maccabee's Jeep. Maybe his Jeep had recently been pimped or something. Or whatever. I wouldn't know; I'm not into cars. "Hey, Mike!" she yelled again.

Mike didn't turn around, but he probably couldn't even hear her above the pounding Chingy track blasting from the Jeep's speakers.

"Meathead," I said to Sonja, who just snapped her gum in response. "Let's go. You can do better—I know it."

"You always say that," said Sonja.

"It's a good thing you have me here, Sonja," I said.

"To raise the bar?" she asked.

"To keep you out of the gutter," I answered.

"And I love you for it," said Sonja.

"Back at you," I said, meaning it.

It was the annual Thomas Jefferson High Schedule Fair, that day a few days before school really starts when we'd all gather in the courtyard to stand in lines and fill out forms and choose electives and join clubs and, more important, get a first look at everyone we hadn't seen all summer. A dry run for the first day of school, in a way . . . and a lickety-split viewing of the year's fresh meat.

"Remember how *into* this we were in ninth grade? All these schedule fairs and pep rallies and football games?" asked Cate, hiking her bag up onto her shoulder. "Now I'd rather just be watching *Judge Judy*."

I lowered my glasses and nodded in agreement. "I heard that," I said. "Don't pee on my leg and tell me it's raining!" I added sternly, one of my favorite Judge Judy lines.

We scaled the small rise that keeps TJ's courtyard hidden from the parking lot out front. Two massive cottonwood trees stood at the top of the rise. Today someone (probably someone in a vice-principal capacity) had strung a huge banner between the two trees. It read, BACK TO TJ: WELCOME HOME.

"Ick," I said as we passed under the sign.

"Be nice," said Sonja. She shook and fluffed her hair. Cate brushed some crumbs off her surf T-shirt and pushed up her shades. I pulled my baseball cap lower over my head.

Below us, streams of students entered the courtyard, ponytails, baseball caps, crew cuts, and cornrows all flowing together. There was a steady, low buzz of conversation, a bubbling mix of, "Omigod! You look great!" and, "Did you get Bosworth for chem?" and, "I heard that Justin guy didn't graduate."

"Okay, you two," said Cate, shaking out her knee. She scanned the courtyard. "If I'm not mistaken, we need to get to that table there. . . ." She squinted and pointed across the yard to a poster that read SENIORS. "That's us. Let's roll. If we lose each other, just text. But no one leaves without the others."

Groaning but prepared, Sonja and I plunged into the crowd behind Cate. We wove our way past the sign-up "stations," which were really just folding card tables adorned with poster-board signs like YEARBOOK WANTS U!! (mobbed, natch, by tenth-grade overachievers) and YOUNG CONSERVATIVES . . . ARE YOU COMMITTED? (manned by two guys in bow ties, one of whom was pretty cute—not that I cared about boys anymore). We passed by CHESS KINGS—CHECKMATE WITH THE CHAMPS! (nerdy) and SWINGIN' SALLY HEMMING'S GOOD-TIME JUKE AND JAZZ BAND (even nerdier).

Cate led, with Sonja just behind her and me tucked in behind Sonja. I wasn't really paying attention to where we were going; I was just following along, trusting Cate to find the place where we were supposed to pick up our paperwork.

"That you, Lucas?" It was Jancee Carmine, TJ's resident party-promoter wannabe and Girl Most Likely to Move to LA and Pursue a Future in Public Relations. Last year I'd set her up with Graham Higgins by switching their identical Nokias. They were still a couple and could often be seen walking around campus together holding hands and talking to other people on their respective cell phones. "Got plans tomorrow?" She dug into her cargo pocket and handed me a flyer, which read, ANNUAL BACK 2 TJ TAILGATER. LAST CHANCE 2 PARTY. "Should be a good time." Her phone, which now hung from a chain around her neck, started to vibrate. "Later," she said, sinking back into the crowd.

"Sonja," I said, turning to her and handing her the flyer. "I believe this is for you."

"What?" said Sonja studying it. "It's a party. Big deal. A tailgater. Who cares?"

"Sonja, I'm surprised at you. Even *I* get it," said Cate. "Maccabee will be there."

"Omigod! Maccabee! You're right!" Sonja squealed and swung her hips. *"Bidi-bidi bom-bom!"*

"Mwah," I replied. "Wear something tight."

"Weren't we going somewhere?" asked Cate, shifting her knapsack to her other shoulder. "Oh yeah, that booth over there." She pointed through the crowd. "Let's go."

After about twenty minutes in line, we managed to sign up and collect our schedules for the year ahead. We each had one elective slot to fill, seventh period. "What's the easiest elective?" Sonja asked as we stepped to the side of the line to read over our papers.

"Music appreciation," I answered.

"Music appreciation? Do you have to stand in line for that?"

"Probably," I answered. "Annoying, huh?"

"Slackers." Cate tsked. "Don't you think you guys should choose your elective based on something other than how easy it is?"

Sonja looked at me. I looked back at her. We both lowered our sunglasses. "Um, no," we said in unison.

"It's our senior elective," I explained. "Slacking is the point."

"Well," said Cate, lowering her own sunglasses. "I'm taking photography, and—"

"And I'm sure Yale and Harvard will just love it on your application, Bonnie Buzzkill," I said. "I'm taking music appreciation."

"Hallelujah," said Sonja, fanning herself with her paperwork.

"Cate, honey, I'm worried about your tendency toward overachievement. Don't you know that excess stress can cause blemishes?"

"Quit exaggerating," said Cate. "Besides, my doctor won't let me play sports this semester. He says my knee needs a few more months to recover from the surgery."

"Yeah, right," said Sonja, turning to me and rolling her eyes. "Where's the line for music . . . music . . . What do you call it?"

"Appreciation," I said. "Music *appreciation*. There." I pointed through a group of overeager underclassmen to the far end of the courtyard. Mr. Abernathy, the teacher, was putting up a sign that read, MUSICIANS BLOW BETTER.

"Perv," said Cate, pushing us toward the booth. "I'm signing up for photo. Cellies on!"

She walked off, limping ever so slightly.

Sonja dragged me through a klatch of cheerleaders. They waved. "Hey, Lucas!"

"Hey!" I yelled back. "You look hot!"

The cheerleaders love me, mostly because I'm gay. As if that were a good enough reason to love someone. They watch *Queer Eye for the Straight Guy* and are always saying stuff like, "Gay guys are so much hotter than straight guys!" and, "Can you take my boyfriend shopping?" and, "Can you take me shopping?" If they only knew what a clueless shopper I am. Just last week I bought girls' sneakers and didn't even know it.

We passed the freaks, headed up by Jenny, Johnny, and

Queen M. They waved from behind a cloud of smoke. "Hey, Lucas! Manson rules!"

"Rock on!" I yelled back, making the sign of the devil with my right hand.

The freaks like me too, ever since me and Johnny and Queen M bonded in a mosh pit during my oh-so-confused Marilyn Manson phase back in tenth grade. Queen M had done my eyeliner for me 'cause I'd had no clue how.

"You'll never be a drag queen," she'd told me. "Which is a shame, 'cause you're pretty."

We passed by a huddle of linebackers on the football team. "Hey, Sonja."

The football players love Sonja. Mostly 'cause of her ass, but also 'cause of her reputation as a guaranteed good time. This, though it would most girls, didn't seem bother her. She waved back, wiggling her assets and smiling slyly. I sized Sonja up—low-slung jeans and piles of hair—and I couldn't tell if I wanted to rescue her or if I wanted to be her.

"There's Maccabee," she said out of the side of her mouth. "Hey, Mike!" she yelled.

"What about Cal, over there?" I pointed to Cal Preston, my chemistry lab partner from last year, who'd just been reinstated to the football team after missing a season because of eligibility requirements. We'd made good lab partners: I told him what to do, and he did it, and we'd scored an A-minus in the class. This made him eligible again and, corny as it sounds, I was sort of proud of him. "He's a good guy. Pretty smart, and I hear he doesn't drink."

"Fun," said Sonja, rolling her eyes.

"Hey, Sonja!" came a voice from behind us. "Hey!"

We turned to see Alex Norita. He was wearing a black turtleneck tucked into pleated khaki shorts. His toes hung over the front of his Tevas. "Welcome back."

"Hi, Alex," I said politely. "We were just talking about you!" I jabbed Sonja. "Weren't we, Sonja?"

Alex marched right up to Sonja. "I hope you have a great year," he said directly and with a smile that was forced but sweet. "See you around, Sonja," he added.

Sonja didn't answer.

"Have a good one, Alex," I said as Alex walked off. "Quit staring, Sonja," I said, teasing her. "Play it cool, or he'll think you're easy."

"Gimme a break, Lucas," said Sonja.

"I'm just saying, Sonja. There's something *there*."

"Maccabee," she growled. "You promised!"

"Okay, you want my help?" I asked. "Fine, take this advice. Mike wants a little bit of a challenge. Quit shaking everything you've got in his face! Make him work for it!"

"How do you know what he wants?" asked Sonja. "You're gay."

"Sonja, you know this: I may be gay, but I'm still a guy. I think like a guy, and I know what guys want."

"Okay, you're right," said Sonja, falling in behind me. "Fine. But how long is it going to take? Like an hour?"

"Sonja," I said. "You're nuts."

"*Mi vida loca,*" she said. "So what are we going to do about Cate?"

"What do you mean?"

"I mean, we have to set her up."

"We? You mean me, don't you, Sonja? You mean *I* have to set her up." I smiled at her.

Sonja just smiled back. "Look, Lucas, Cate's got to get over Vince once and for all," she said. "And you are the master."

I rolled my eyes, but I knew Sonja was right. Cate did have to be set up. And she'd been so cool over the last week, helping me get through the whole Marcus thing. I'd practically spent the entire weekend on her couch, watching a Bollywood-a-thon on channel 73 and throwing Tater Tots in the Fry Daddy. Sonja came over and the three of us drank coffee with Bailey's in it and made a dos leches cake because we didn't have all the ingredients for a tres leches cake. We barely talked about Marcus or Vince all weekend—I didn't know what to say, and Cate didn't force me—and it was perfect. Sometimes it's not about talking it out. Sometimes it's just about enduring. The first few days always suck, and Cate made sure I made it through. Once again, she'd saved me from completely losing it.

"Sonja, you're right." I readjusted my sunglasses and scanned the crowd. "Look around. There's got to be someone. Who's new this year? Who got cute over the summer? Remember, she likes tall, tan boys with varsity letters and sandy hair. We've got to find The Hottest Guy Ever."

I barely felt Sonja kicking me on the ankle. "Lucas!"

But I was still talking. "Maybe we should pick people by their SAT scores. 'Cause he's gotta be smart," I said. "Cate's dated too many dumb guys. But he can't be an overachiever. We need someone laid back. Maybe an artist. Not an actor."

"Lucas!" Another kick. "Hotness, twelve o'clock." Sonja pointed to a figure near the front of the music appreciation line. "How about that for heat?"

I inhaled sharply. "Wow," I muttered, pushing down my sunglasses to take in the vision before me. "Wow."

The vision had dirty-blond hair falling into his face. He wore a faded yellow T-shirt that was just this side of too tight and said ANDREWS SUGAR SHACK, SAUGERTIES, NEW YORK. No sunglasses. Strong profile, heavy nose. Squinty eyes with big eyelashes that I could see even from this far away. A great big sports bag that said UMBRO. Adidas turf shoes. *A soccer player?* A diving watch. Blond hair on his forearms.

"It's him," said Sonja. "The Hottest Guy Ever."

The Hottest Guy Ever then released his lip from his teeth and stretched his arms over his head. Sonja gasped. (Or was that me?) He had on the best-fitting faded jeans I'd ever seen. Somewhere between dark and light blue, with a tiny rip at the knee, they were just beginning to fray at the waist. One belt loop had been torn off. I wondered how that had happened. The denim was slightly loose at the thigh but fitted enough to hint at muscles underneath. Soccer-player legs?

This was too perfect, like some kind of sign. My mission was clear. Now he was at the front of the line.

The Hottest Guy Ever smiled at Mr. Abernathy, who snapped his treble-clef-decorated suspenders and said,

"Sorry, my friend, we're all filled up! Welcome to TJ! Try ceramics!" He pointed to a clipboard on the table directly adjacent to his. "I hear a few spots are open there!" And then he laughed like this was the funniest thing in the world.

"Thanks," said The Hottest Guy Ever, shaking his head slightly. He walked three steps to the right, leaned down, and signed his name on the ceramics list. Then he turned and walked back into the crowd, grazing Sonja's shoulder as he stepped past. Not in a klutzy way, but almost like he'd meant to.

"Sorry," he said, smiling and reaching around Sonja's waist to steady her. "Are you okay?"

Sonja stood still, smiling. THGE, staring into Sonja's eyes, took a step back, coming down hard on my left foot. I snapped back and grabbed at my toe. "Ouch!"

He spun around and reached around my shoulders to steady me. His hands were strong and warm, and I felt a shock. "Sorry, man," said THGE. "It's my first day here." He smiled apologetically, eyes green and bright. "Hey, do you know where the soccer field is? I have to be there by two."

"That way," I answered blankly, pointing to my right. I could not stop staring at his jaw. It was so square. "Past the parking lot."

"Thanks, man." He smiled as he folded himself into the crowd. "See you around."

He called me "man."

"Wow," said Sonja, gazing after him. "Check out the jeans from the back."

"Perfect," I said dreamily. I wondered what THGE had eaten for breakfast that morning. And whether he'd washed his hair today or if he'd skipped it. I wondered what he slept in. I wondered if he was in love. I wondered if his heart had ever been broken. I wanted to fix it for him. Suddenly I didn't care what his SAT scores were.

Sonja cut to the front of the line to check the list for Mr. Hottest's name. "Derek Griffin," she said, turning back to me. "Screw Mike Maccabee. I want Derek."

"Forget it," I said, snapping out of my dream before it went too far. Hot guys always get me depressed. My fantasies never play out the way I want them to. So I've learned to cut them short. It's a lot easier than trying to make them happen, which is a hobby for suckers. "He's Cate's, and you know I'm right."

"Did you see his ass?" she asked, licking her lips.

"Take it easy, Darcy Desperate," I warned. "Think of Cate."

Sonja looked wistfully at Derek for another second, then grabbed my arm. She nodded. "Cate has to switch her elective to ceramics now! Let's find her, quick. Before she gets stuck taking photo!"

"You're reading my mind," I said as we started to make our way through the crowd.

We found Cate at the front of the line at the photo booth, shaking a pen to get the ink flowing so she could sign up for the class. "Stop!" yelled Sonja. "Don't do it!"

Cate turned so fast her wraparounds flew off her head. "What? What happened?"

I smacked Sonja on the head. "Don't freak her out!"

Sonja smacked back. "Watch the hair!"

I took Cate by the arm. "Cate, nothing happened. But we strongly believe that you should consider taking ceramics as your elective. We have some important information that we think may help you make up your mind." I took the pen out of her hand.

"What are you talking about?" said Cate. She was looking at us like we were crazy. "Ceramics? Huh?"

"Are you signing up or what?" said the guy who was standing in line behind Cate. "I have to get to a band meeting. We need to practice our beats."

"Beat something else for a minute," said Sonja, waving him away. "Cate, look." She pointed into the crowd.

As if by magic, the courtyard cleared right where Sonja was pointing. There, directly under a spotlight-sunbeam so golden and bright that it made everyone else look like they were standing in shadows, stood Derek Griffin. Even hotter than before. He looked down at his handful of papers, then up over the milling crowd in one direction, then another, squinting to read the signs over the tables surrounding the courtyard. Even from here I could see that bleach-blond hair on his forearms and the green glint in his eyes.

"Derek Griffin," I muttered in Cate's ear. "And he's taking ceramics. Now, weren't you saying that you wanted to learn how to make a nice clay ashtray too?" I put my arm around her shoulders.

"Wow," said Cate. Her eyes flickered, and she half smiled.

"My thoughts exactly."

Just then Derek glanced up from his stack of papers and looked directly at us. I wondered if our tongues were hanging out.

"You two are crazy," said Cate, the first to break the moment. "I don't even know who this guy is. And neither, by the way, do you. Do you even know what grade he's in?" Cate bent down to pick up her sunglasses.

"Well, we know that he's hot," said Sonja.

"Do you even know if he's single?" asked Cate.

"Look who's full of questions!" said Sonja. "Someone is interested! At least we know he's straight. Check out those turf shoes and that soccer bag."

"Sonja, what century are you in? Turf shoes have nothing to do with anyone being straight or gay. Right, Lucas?"

It was the first time it had even occurred to me to consider that Derek could be anything *but* straight.

"He's probably straight. I mean, most of you people are, right?" I was bewildered, buzzing.

"See?" said Sonja. "Lucas agrees. So come sign up for clay class."

"Forget it," said Cate. "Give me that pen." She signed up for photography. Except I wasn't going to forget it. Not by a long shot. Getting Cate together with Derek wasn't going to be easy, but I always liked a challenge. Besides, I needed to keep myself busy, since I wouldn't be dating anyone myself. This seemed a worthwhile way to spend the next few weeks. And Cate would love me in the end.

Step one: Find out more about Mr. Hot. I mean Derek.

3.

Friday

"DO YOU SEE HIM ANYWHERE?" I ASKED SONJA AS WE approached the soccer field, crowded with players doing wind sprints between the midfield lines, everyone breathing heavily. "We need to know if those turf shoes were just for show."

"Wow," said Sonja. "You didn't tell me they'd all be in shorts."

"Breathe," I said.

I saw Cate sitting on the sidelines. "Hey! What's up?"

"Just checking out the team," said Cate. "I think Julian's really going to stand out this year." She pointed to where her younger brother, one of the stars of the team, was doing frog jumps with a few other players at the far goal line. For a brother and sister they were especially close, and Cate adored him. "He's just getting stronger," she said, sounding proud. She waved to him, and he broke from the pack, jogging slowly toward us.

"So, Cate," I asked, sitting next to her on the grass. "Wish you were out there?" Cate hadn't played soccer since last spring, when she'd torn a tendon in her knee during a practice session. It was this injury that had led to her surgery over the summer, a tendon graft. Not major, but delicate.

"Nah," she said, shaking her knee.

"Liar," I said, smiling.

Julian jogged up wearing a Brook/Lyn sweatshirt and shiny soccer shorts. He was smiling and dribbling a soccer ball with his feet. "Well, it doesn't matter, because Dr. Bao said you can't kick a ball again until March," he said. "Remember?"

"Hey, Julian," said Sonja.

"Hey, Julian," I said. "Looking good out there."

"Hey, Sonja. Hey, Lucas," said Julian, kicking the soccer ball up, and then tossing it from hand to hand. "Thanks, man," he said to me.

"It's soccer," said Sonja. "I thought you weren't supposed to use your hands."

"I'm the goalie," said Julian, bouncing from foot to foot. Whenever there was a soccer ball around, Julian was in constant motion.

"Oh," said Sonja. "Whatever. Anyway, nice crew cut."

"Thanks," said Julian, rubbing the top of his freshly shorn head and dropping his gaze. Julian was a perfect boy-version of Cate: He had the same blond hair, the same wide green eyes, the same baby face. And that one crooked tooth that you could only see when he smiled.

"Looking good out there," said Cate as she reached over to scratch Julian's head. "Did you stretch out this morning?"

"Yes, Mom," said Julian, swatting her hand away playfully. "I stretched." He stuck out his leg and bent it back and forth. "See? Flexible."

"Good," said Cate. "Don't screw it up like mine. We Sawyers have bad knees." Cate was hard on herself about her knee, which she believed she wouldn't have injured if she'd stretched it out better. "Promise."

Suddenly, from beyond the goal where Julian had been standing, a figure came racing toward the field, tapping a soccer ball from foot to foot as he ran. It was Derek. His legs were muscled, long, and moving speedily, delicately, powerfully. The ball danced against his toes. I was transfixed and forgot for a moment where I was or why.

So he *was* on the team. And not only that, he looked like he knew what he was doing.

"Mmm," said Sonja.

"That's Derek," I heard Julian saying. "He's supposedly really good, but I haven't seen him play yet. He's from New York or New Jersey or something." Julian started bouncing the ball from toe to toe.

"They say he was the high scorer on his team last year."

Cate, still on the grass, held her arms up. Julian tossed her the ball, which she caught and spun between her hands. Her eyes followed Derek out onto the field.

"Well, is he single?" asked Sonja.

"I have no idea," responded Julian. "Why?" He grabbed

at the ball in Cate's hand. "Here comes Coach. I better go. See you guys later." He picked up the ball and tossed it in the air. He bounced it off his head as he trotted back out onto the grass.

"Get a load of that ass," muttered Sonja.

Cate smacked her on the shoulder. "Sonja! That is my brother!"

"I wasn't talking about your brother," said Sonja, pointing at Derek, who was now deftly heading the ball back and forth with Julian. "I was talking about your future boyfriend."

Cate and I followed Sonja's gaze out to the field. Just then, Julian jumped for the ball and landed hard, his leg crumpling underneath him. He dropped to the ground with an audible thud. Sonja and I gasped. Cate shrieked, "Julian!"

Derek, who'd just taken the shot that Julian had been diving for, sprinted to Julian's side, extending his arm. "Dude!" he yelled. "Are you okay?"

Cate jump-started, sprinting onto the field. "Julian!" she cried.

"I'm okay," Julian called, reaching for Derek's hand and pulling himself up. "Cate! Don't run!"

Cate slowed to a jog.

I stood, watching Derek. He pulled Julian to his feet, then took him by both shoulders and looked square into his eyes. I was at least forty yards away, so I couldn't hear what they were saying, if they were saying anything. But Derek wrapped one arm around Julian's neck and rubbed his crew cut with the other. They wrestled for a second; then Derek tapped Julian sharply on the butt and sprinted away.

I gulped, suddenly anxious. *What would that feel like?*

Cate was still several paces from Julian, walking slowly now, limping, but still approaching. "It's cool, *Mom*," he teased her, jogging over to show her. "See? I'm fine. Don't worry."

"Okay," said Cate, stopping. She turned, dropped her eyes, and walked carefully back toward me and Sonja. "I'm crazy." She shook her head.

Sonja held out her arms to hug Cate. "It's okay," she said. "You're not crazy. He's your baby."

"Yes," said Cate. "And I'm his mommy." She caught her breath. "Someone needs to be."

I'd known Cate for more than ten years now, and I'd only seen her mother once, when she'd come out of her room to tell us to turn down the TV. Mrs. Sawyer spent most of her time in bed, sick. Or drunk, depending on who you asked. And I'd never seen Mr. Sawyer, who was always in Toronto, where he worked for some bottled water company. For the last few years, it seemed like Cate and Julian had pretty much raised themselves.

Cate turned back to look at the field just in time to see Derek head the ball past Julian into the top corner of the goal. "He is pretty good, you know."

"Julian?" I asked. "Yup, he's amazing." And he always had been. Back in elementary school I'd played two seasons of Peewee soccer on the Cook Park Kickapoo team. Julian, though a year younger, had been on the Observatory Park Hopi team. I remembered being kind of impressed because he was the only kid in the whole league who'd been able to bounce the ball on his head ten consecutive times. He was way better than me. Not that I was that bad; I just wasn't that interested.

"No, I mean Derek," said Cate. "He's good." She nodded toward him, standing with a group of players at midfield. "Did you see how he took care of Julian back there?"

"Yeah," I said. "I did see that. It was almost romantic."

"I know, they're so cute together," joked Sonja.

"Very funny." Cate laughed, turning back to the field just in time to see Derek steal the ball from another player. "Very funny."

"She's blushing," said Sonja, snapping in the air.

I lowered my sunglasses. True enough, Cate was in full blush. Too easy to read. "Totally blushing." *Damn. She likes him.*

"You guys need hobbies," said Cate, half smiling. "Let's get out of here."

We turned away from the field just in time to see Vince jogging toward us, shirtless in sweatpants. He was grinning, somewhere in that facial hair: two superthin lines that started as his sideburns, then traced their way down his jawline as far as his chin, then turned, sharp, to his mouth, where they wound themselves into a pencil mustache.

"Looks like someone just got the latest issue of *Goatee*

Art magazine," I muttered to Sonja, who was busy staring at Vince's rapidly approaching abs.

"What's up, Catie?" said Vince, raising his arms over his head.

"Get lost," said Cate, staring at the ground. The color of her blush had gone from embarrassed to pissed.

"You don't have to hate on me," said Vince, snapping his T-shirt over one shoulder, then the other. "I'm not that bad."

"I believe," said Sonja, arching her back and waving her finger in the air, "that Cate just asked you to leave."

"Was I talking to you?" Vince taunted Sonja. "No. I was talking to Cate. Wasn't I, Cate?"

"Haven't you heard?" demanded Sonja. "Cate's moved on."

"Moved on?" scoffed Vince. "Moved on with who?"

I grabbed Cate's arm. "Sonja!" I gasped. "Shut up!"

"None of your business, Vince," said Sonja, lunging at Vince to push him away.

"Ooh, spunky," hissed Vince. "Uncle Vinnie likes that in a girl." He dodged her lunge and started jogging off. "Call me when you're ready for some of this, Sonja," he spat, grabbing his crotch.

"Screw you, Vince." Sonja sighed and dropped her voice. "But your abs look fine today."

"I hate him," said Cate, turning stiffly and walking toward the car.

"Me too," I said.

"All the more reason to get with Derek," said Sonja. "Show that boy what a man really is."

We walked back to the parking lot in silence, Cate leading, shoulders squared, determined. Her limp was nowhere to be seen, and her pace was hard to match without jogging. Sonja and I trotted along a step or two behind.

As we reached the edge of the parking lot, Cate slowed her pace for several steps, then turned around for one last wave at Julian, who waved back.

Derek waved too.

"He seems like a pretty good guy," said Cate. "Derek, I mean."

"I noticed," I said, because I had.

"I could like someone like that," she said.

"I bet you could," I said. "What's not to like?"

"Is that tailgater tonight?" asked Cate, stroking her chin as if she had a beard.

"Yup," I answered, half amazed and half panicked by how quickly and easily this match was coming together. "Everyone will be there."

"Why don't you and Sonja come pick me up around eight?"

4.

Friday

Bidi-bidi bom-bom! went Sonja's Selena ring tone. She looked at the caller ID on her phone. She squinted at the number, then shrugged. She flipped open her phone. "*¿Dígame?*" she demanded, switching to Spanish. This was something she did whenever she didn't recognize the number of the person calling her.

"*¿Quién? ¡No! ¡No entiendo!*" she yelled into the phone. She hung up, then looked at me. "I can't believe you actually gave Alex Norita my number!"

"Maybe I did, maybe I didn't," I deadpanned. The truth was, I actually hadn't. It had never even occurred to me. Alex Norita could hack his way to any phone number he wanted to. He was a notoriously adept computer whiz, even getting busted last year for "exposing weaknesses" in the school's security system (i.e., hacking into the mainframe and posting a fake "official school item" about how

Lieutenant Uhura was being installed as vice principal). This had made him a minor antihero at school, but he was still solidly in the nerd category.

I was pretty impressed that he'd had the balls to call Sonja. "So that was . . . ?"

"Yes, that was Alex Norita. A very confused Alex Norita who clearly had the *wrong number*."

"Oh, Lord," I said, laughing. "You could at least be nice to him!"

"I'll get you," said Sonja, holding her palm in my face. "This has you written all over it." She slipped back behind the Chinese screen that blocked off the far end of the living room, creating my mom's "bedroom." Sonja was helping Mom pick an outfit for tonight's date. She'd recently lost twelve pounds on South Beach and had been all over Match.com. Tonight was her third first date in two weeks.

"I don't know, Sonja," I heard Mom saying. "This seems a little short." I imagined Mom tugging at her hemline. "Don't you think it seems a little short?"

"Oh, please, Audrey!" scolded Sonja. "It's supposed to be short. In fact, hike it up! Check out those legs!"

Mom walked out from behind the screen, fluffing her pageboy and smoothing out the front of her skirt. "What do you think, Lucas? Do you think he'll like this? Do I look like a ho?"

"Please don't say that, Mom," I answered. "Mothers aren't supposed to use the term *ho*. It's disturbing."

"Oh, relax, Lucas," she said. "I'm hip."

Ever since the divorce, it had just been her and me in this apartment. We'd done pretty well. She was my mom; I was her son. Easy. But when I told her I like guys, things changed. Suddenly it was like I was a different person to her, some huge mystery that she couldn't relate to no matter how hard she tried—and she tried way too hard. You know . . . trendy outfits, slang, asking who I thought was hot. She started dating, a lot, and sharing the details with me. She stopped acting like a mother, trying to act like my friend instead, like a peer. It was weird. I mean, I had friends already. I liked her better as my mother.

But I suppose she didn't know what else to do. It sucked for her, I'm sure. I mean, no one exactly *wants* their kid to be gay. No one celebrates when their kid comes out of the closet. There's no cake. There's no gifts. It's not something you call your friends to brag about.

I wondered, sometimes, if all her dating lately was some kind of weird psychological thing, like she was hoping to meet a new man and have another son, this one not gay. I guess it was a good thing that she had me so young. She still had time.

I did want Mom to be happy; I was just hoping she wouldn't find anyone until after I graduated. The last thing I needed was some *man* in the house.

"Whatcha think?" said Mom, waving a printed page in front of me. "He's pretty cute, huh?" She pointed to a head shot of a man who appeared to be in his mid-forties, with receding hair and an aggressive, toothy smile. He looked like he'd just spent the day in the sun with no SPF, unless he was just naturally the color of a lobster.

"Uh . . ." I said, wishing I didn't have to have this conversation with my mother. "Not my type."

Mom, who wasn't paying attention anyway, turned back to the screen. "But what about the skirt? Do you think it's too short? I don't know what to wear!"

"Sonja!" I moaned. "Rescue me!"

"Trust me, Audrey," said Sonja, coming out from behind the screen. "Who cares if people think you're a ho? You know who you are. Wear it. And wear the red shoes," Sonja added. "You're at your sexual peak. Look like it!"

"It's true," said Mom. "Sex now is better than I ever imagined it would be. I've really started taking responsibility for my own fulfillment, and it makes all the difference."

"Ack," I gagged, flipping the channels. "Now I'm truly nauseous." That was another thing that had happened once I told my mother that I was gay—all of a sudden, her sex life was like an open topic of conversation.

"Take it easy, Lucas," said Mom. "We're just having some girl talk."

Girl talk. Whatever. No thanks. Leave me out of it.

Just then, a horn sounded from out front. "That's him! My date!" yelled Mom, scrambling behind the screen. "Sonja, where's my lip gloss?"

"He doesn't come to the door?" I complained from the couch. "What kind of guy is this? Did he at least shower for you?"

"Here!" Sonja tossed her a tube of lip gloss. "Take mine!"

"Don't wait up!" chirped Mom, grabbing her purse from the coffee table and dashing out the door.

"Lip gloss?" I asked.

"Relax," said Sonja. "It's cute. She's fine. Besides, she's letting you borrow her car tonight. Speaking of which, what are *you* going to wear?"

"I don't care," I lied, flipping the channel. I really did care.

"Hey, *mijo*!" She snatched the remote out of my hand, turning off the TV. "We're about to go to a party. Smiles! It's going to be fun!" Sonja kicked my feet off the coffee table. "Come on!"

"Take it easy, Susie Sunshine. It's a tailgate party."

"Oh, excuse me, Puffy. I'm sorry we can't party in the champagne room with Paris and Nicole tonight. Get off the couch."

I got off the couch.

After dressing me in a pair of carpenter jeans, a long-sleeved surfer tee, and black-and-white Adidas, Sonja and I stopped by Cate's for a couple of Cokes. They had theirs with rum. I, as designated driver, had mine without. Then Cate, Sonja, Julian, and I all buckled ourselves into Mom's Subaru and headed for the tailgater.

I knew what to expect before we got there. Funnels of Coors, bad pop-punk on someone's over-bassed car stereo, freak dancing, maniacal drunken laughter, hysterical drunken crying, and lots of talk about backseat hand jobs. Another big Friday night in Denver.

I drove the Subaru into the mostly dark parking lot and pulled into a spot, which I noticed was just a few spaces away from Vince's Mustang.

"Thanks for the lift," said Julian. He climbed out, shook a stone out of his Birkenstock, and wandered over to the party, which was clustered under the only working streetlight in the parking lot. It was a bustling pit of baseball caps, cargo shorts, and flip-flops, this year's required Abercrombie Wannacrombie uniform for both boys and girls. "Julian!" someone yelled. "Get wasted!"

"Oh, God. We better get over there," said Cate. "Before they eat him alive." She reached for her baseball cap, which was sitting on the backseat. She pulled it over her head, threading her ponytail through the back. "There."

Sonja grabbed at Cate's baseball cap. "Take that off."

"Quit it, you retard!" teased Cate. "My hair sucks."

"You white girls don't understand hair," said Sonja, shaking out her own locks. "Boys like it long."

"You would know," said Cate, smiling and jabbing at Sonja. Cate tightened her ponytail.

"You guys done?" I asked.

"Paaaarty!!" yelled Sonja. She hiked down her jeans, adjusted the straps of her camisole top, tossed her hair, and made a beeline for the pickup truck in the middle of the baseball cap pit. Halfway there, she threw her arms over her head, turned, and shouted, "Without you, I'm nothing!" She turned back and bounced toward the party, flipping her hair.

"Woo-hoo! Beer me! Hey, Mike!"

"Sonja!" I hissed. "Make him work for it!"

She didn't turn around.

"Is that the last we'll be seeing of Sonja tonight?" asked Cate, shaking her head.

"Probably," I answered, tapping her baseball cap.

"I don't know how she does it," said Cate.

"Away we go," I said.

I didn't really want to be here, but I knew I had to be. I mean, you couldn't just miss the first tailgater of the year. If I didn't at least show my face, I'd have to hear about it all through the first day of school. "Where *were* you? You missed a *great* party!"

We strolled over toward the thick of the party, which by now was about fifty people strong. "Hey, Lucas!" shouted Cassandra Castillo, this year's most likely candidate for head cheerleader and one of my recent setup subjects. "Did you see *Will & Grace* last night?" She was standing with a couple of lesser cheerleaders near the pickup, all of them in doubled-up tank tops in contrasting colors. They were sharing a cigarette.

"Hey, Cassandra," I said, walking over to give her an air kiss. "I missed it. Was it good? Your hair looks great." She'd obviously had a tussle with Miss Clairol recently, and her hair was about four different shades of ash.

"Thanks. My streaks are still settling in," she said, flipping it. "Lucas, I always think of you when I see *Will & Grace*! Don't you just loooooove Jack?"

"Yeah," I answered, biting my tongue to hold back what

I really wanted to say, which was that I never understood why they didn't just give Will a dachshund. From what I could tell, Jack served the same purpose.

"Oh hi, Cate!" chirped Cassandra over my shoulder. "I didn't see you there!"

Cate waved back, wiggling her fingers in the air. "Hi, Cassandra."

"So, you heard the news?" said Cassandra, leaning in. "Brandon and I are . . ." She trailed off, then drew her finger across her throat. "Over."

"Yeah, I heard," I said, which wasn't true. I hadn't heard. But I wasn't surprised. I'd known when I switched seats with her so she could sit next to Hummer-driving varsity baseball star Brandon in English class last semester that it wouldn't last.

"Well," I said, "don't feel too bad about it. He was a placeholder. And you had fun, right?"

"Totally," she said. "Loved the car. But I was maxed out on him by June. Anyway, sniff, I'm single again. Can you *believe* it?"

"Say it isn't so," I said, winking at her. "You? Single? No way."

"You'll help me though, right?" She gave me a hopeful smile.

I looked around. "I won't rest until we resolve this!" I said with forced enthusiasm. "But first I need a drink." There'd been a time about a year ago when I'd really cherished my role as matchmaker. I'd loved taking two lonely people and helping make them happy with each other. And making them feel good made me feel good. And important. Lately I was having trouble getting as excited about it as I used to—the thrill had worn off or something. And most of the relationships didn't last anyway. But everyone still expected me to be TJ's answer to Cupid (but thinner and less naked). I hated to disappoint.

"Lucas," she squealed, bouncing and hugging me at the same time while I struggled to stand solidly. "I just loooooove you!!" She slobbered all over my cheek.

"Back at ya." I smiled.

Cate grabbed my arm and yanked me away toward the pickup truck with the cooler on the tailgate. "Lucas," she whispered, "I just *looooove* you!" She crossed her eyes all googly. "Cheerleaders," she scoffed.

"Be nice!" I scolded. "Don't be such a snob. Cassandra's okay, even if she is a cheerleader. We must be tolerant of diversity, remember?"

She rolled her eyes. "Want a beer?"

"Uh, designated driver!" I pointed to myself.

"Grrr," she growled, reaching into the cooler. She produced one Coors Light and a Coke. We popped open the tops and tried to clink them together, only cans don't clink. "Cheers."

I scanned the crowd, searching, if I were to be honest with myself, for Derek. I guessed that Cate, also making a visual sweep of the crowd, was doing the same thing. But I didn't ask. She'd deny it anyway.

53

At first glance, I didn't see Derek anywhere. I spotted Julian playing with his hacky sack next to my car, alone. I saw Sonja, trying to work her way through the klatch of football players to Mike Maccabee, who was right in the middle. I saw Vince holding up a funnel for some girl I didn't recognize (a freshman?) and chanting, "Chug! Chug! Chug!"

There was a tap on my shoulder. "Hey, Lucas." It was Alex Norita, in a black turtleneck tucked into jean shorts. His glasses were foggy. "What's up?" he asked. I was surprised to see him here, but Alex Norita was full of surprises. For a geek, he was amazingly confident.

"Hey, Alex. Nothing much," I answered. "You know, just chilling. Tailgater and all!"

"Are you taking microbio this year?"

"Nope," I said. "I'm doing physics instead."

"My dad's making me do micro. He says I have to be a doctor. Every first boy in our family is a doctor." He rolled his eyes.

"Parents," I said, "have issues."

Cate snorted; I smiled. Alex just looked at us quizzically.

"Have you seen Sonja tonight?" he asked.

Cate elbowed me.

"Yes," I said. "She's here somewhere." I looked around so I could point her out. Unfortunately, there she was, freak dancing with two of Mike Maccabee's friends while Mike chatted with another girl, a short, skinny blonde I didn't recognize.

"Um," I said. "I, uh . . ."

"Oh, there she is," said Alex. He cast his eyes down for a moment, then shrugged. "Well, maybe I can catch her later." He thrust his hands into his pockets and walked away from the crowd.

"This is quite a party so far," said Cate. "Sonja appears to be spoken for. So can't we leave?"

"Not yet," I answered. "We have more to do." We needed to find Derek. For Cate.

"Hey," came a deep voice from behind us. I stepped to the side, turned to see who was talking, and gasped.

There stood Derek, all six feet of him, blond-forearmed, faded-jeaned, and turf-shoed. In this light, a combo of starlight, flickering streetlight, and pickup headlights, he was amazing. The light made the angles in his face sharp, the shadows under his eyebrows dark. "I recognize you," he said, staring intently at my face. "Weren't you at soccer today?"

His jeans were baggy and slung low, revealing a sharp shadow beneath his hip bone.

Blinking, I looked up to see the photo-print stretched across his T-shirt . . . a picture of a Weimaraner in a pair of sunglasses talking on a phone.

"Was that you?"

Snap! Wake up, Lucas. Stop! He's talking to you! "I'm— I'm sorry," I stammered. "Was who me?" I looked over at Cate for support, but she was just staring at Derek dreamily.

"At soccer," he repeated. "Today." He turned to Cate. "And you were there too. Aren't you Julian's friend? I saw you on the field today. He kept calling you 'Mom,' but you don't look like a mom."

"Sister," answered Cate, snapping out of her dreaminess and into the direct and confident tone she always had when talking about Julian. "I'm his sister."

"Ah, mystery solved," said Derek. "Finally."

Mystery? I thought. *Finally?* Had he been wondering about us all day? *I mean,* I corrected myself, *wondering about Cate?* I needed to switch off this moment before it went too far. The last thing I needed was a crush on Derek, when I was already determined to set him up with Cate.

"Wegman," said Cate, pointing at Derek's T-shirt. "I love him."

"Yup, William Wegman," said Derek. "He's my favorite photographer. My name is Derek." He held out his hand to shake hers. For all we'd talked about him, I was surprised to realize that we hadn't actually met him before. "I'm new to TJ. I just moved here from New York."

"Cate," she said. "And this is Lucas."

"Hi, Lucas," he said, extending his hand. His grip was strong and warm but not too firm. "Do you play soccer too?"

"No," I said. "But Cate here does. In fact, she taught Julian everything he knows."

"Really?" said Derek, sounding genuinely impressed. "You must be a great teacher, 'cause that kid is good."

"Well." Cate smiled and shook her head. "We just kick the ball around sometimes, you know?"

"She's been varsity two years running," I said. "Cate here is a star."

"Not like Julian," protested Cate. "He's a real star."

"You should have seen some of the saves Julian made today," offered Derek, emptying his last sip of beer into his mouth. "I'm just glad he's on my team so I don't have to try to score against him."

"You should be," said Cate, smiling coyly. "He had three scoreless games last year as a sophomore. But maybe he's met his match." Was she *flirting*?

"What about you?" asked Derek. "What was your record?" He wiped the side of his mouth with his forearm, stretching his lip across his teeth, sexy.

"We were 10–4 on the season," said Cate matter-of-factly. "And we took second at districts."

"Nice," he said. "That's a great record." He leaned in and lowered his voice. "But how did you do in Pueblo?"

Cate looked at him, impressed. The annual statewide round-robin soccer tournaments were held in Pueblo twice a year: autumn for boys, spring for girls. "You know about Pueblo?"

"Yeah," said Derek, grinning widely. "I hear that the final there is, like, the game of the year, that your record doesn't even really matter. All that matters is Pueblo. Is that true?" He pushed his hair back from his face with his left hand only for it to flop right back. *Marcus used to do that.*

I had to get out of there. I had to stop staring. I had to leave them alone. I did not need a crush to confuse me. Not now. Not after Marcus. Not yet. Maybe not ever.

"Derek, is it?" I said, craning my head around. "I gotta pee. I'll be back. Can you look after Cate?"

"Lucas!" said Cate.

"I'll be back," I said. "You're fine," I whispered. I took her hand and gave it a quick squeeze.

"Hurry back," said Derek, holding up his beer and biting his lower lip.

Flushed, I turned and wandered into the emptiest corner of the parking lot, over by Mom's Subaru. I heard Sonja's laugh and saw her on the hood of Mike Maccabee's truck. She was talking to two of Mike's friends, but not to Mike, who had his arm around the short, skinny blonde. I stole a glance or two back at Derek and Cate, who were chatting comfortably, probably about soccer. I saw Derek reach over and tap Cate's baseball cap, flirting, and my eyelids flickered with a mix of envy, avarice, and lust. That was three deadly sins right there.

But I could keep this crush at bay. I'd done it before. For years I'd been clipping off fantasies, stopping them short, saving myself the disappointment. Lust management. It's a survival skill.

Sure, Derek was hot, but so what? He wasn't the first cute guy I'd never get, or the last. And sure, so he seemed genuinely nice and cool; so what? And there was an extra something in his eyes that . . . *Stop,* I told myself. The ache I was feeling right now would fade. It always did.

I kept walking. I'd just go chill out in the Subaru and listen to music for a while, then maybe gather the girls and head home. I came upon my car to find Julian sprawled across the hood on his back, hands behind his head. His

Birkenstocks had fallen to the ground. "Dude," I said, "what are you doing?"

"Nothing," he said, not sitting up. "Just looking at the stars." Julian spoke slowly, like he always did off the field. During a practice or a game, his focus was searing. But off the field, Julian was quiet. He had a lazy way about him. Not sad, just a little sleepy. He always seemed like he'd just been woken up. I liked it.

"That's it? All alone? Aren't you bored?" I asked. "I mean, it's a bunch of stars, just hanging there. What's the big deal?"

"Nah," said Julian. "I'm looking at the stars. That's not boring."

Was this weird or cute or what? I couldn't decide.

"You should check this out," said Julian.

"What?" I asked. "Check what out?"

"The view," he said, pointing to the sky. "It's perfect."

"Amazing," I said cynically. "Stars." Was he *stoned*?

"No," said Julian, raising his head and looking at me. "You have to get on your back." He shifted his body to one side of the hood and patted the spot next to him. "Come lie here. It's a perfect night for stars and perfect that we're here, away from the light."

I knew I had nothing better to do at the moment. I sat up on the hood and lay back. "Okay," I said. "Stars."

"Okay, now take deep, slow breaths," said Julian. "And don't focus on any one star. Let your eyes relax and let them all blend together."

I looked over at the party, where I could see some guy pouring a beer onto Sonja's back. God, I hated Denver.

I relaxed my eyes. The stars went from a bunch of shiny white spots in the sky to a mist, moving and alive, like billion-mile spray paint splattered out in every direction. Suddenly the party, Derek, and everything else faded into the background.

"You're right," I said. "It's beautiful. Thanks."

"Anytime," said Julian. "Anytime."

Neither one of us said another word. I'm not sure how long we lay there. But I just stared at the stars and tried hard not to think about Derek, the hot, nice, cool, interesting new soccer player from New York.

5.

Saturday

IT WASN'T UNTIL WELL AFTER TEN, WHEN I WAS IDLING AWAY IN the Burger King drive-through, that I realized I was still in my pajama pants. I really needed this cup of coffee and Croissan'wich.

I readjusted my Mets cap, pulling it down low, while I fiddled with the Subaru radio, landing on a weather report. "Another perfect Colorado day! We are at seventy-three degrees presently under sunny skies. We expect a high this afternoon of eighty-five under partial cloud cover. Watch for scattered thunderstorms around six, but they'll only stick around for an hour or so. All will be clear for your evening barbecue. Have a great day!"

I tried not to scowl. *Another perfect Colorado day.* Zzzz. I wanted them to announce a massive storm front. A hailstorm, maybe, with a tornado or two.

The line started to move, so I took my foot off the brake to crawl along. I was wondering whether the Burger King would survive a direct hit by a tornado or whether the Subaru would, when the red Volvo station wagon in front of me stalled and stopped short. I slammed on the brakes.

SCREECH!

Only I didn't hit the brake fast enough, and in a flash, my bumper clipped the back of the Volvo, bouncing me in my seat.

Then *BAM!* again. Stronger this time, harder. I knew immediately that I'd been hit from behind. I reached for my license.

I heard the door on the car behind me open and slam and an all-too-familiar voice shouting, approaching, "Hey, loser! Nice going!"

And there was Vince in my rearview mirror, walking around the front of his Mustang, bending down to look at his bumper. His face was bright red. "What the hell? I can't *believe* this! This car is *cherry!*"

I pulled my Mets cap down again farther as he walked up to my window. I turned to see him spit. "No way. It's *you.*"

Where was Sonja when I needed her?

I inhaled and braced myself. "It wasn't my fault," I mumbled, unbuckling my seat belt. I opened the car door right into Vince, accidentally-on-purpose hitting him on the leg. He jumped back, losing a flip-flop. "Watch it!" he yelled. "Fag!"

I heard a couple of guys in the parking lot snicker as I got out of the car. *Great,* I thought. *An audience.*

"Sorry," I said without looking up from under my cap, staying low.

I kept breathing, looking down. Vince paced in a little circle, still cussing.

Then, from the corner of my eye, I noticed the Volvo's driver approaching. I didn't raise my eyes, assuming the worst.

All I could see from under my cap were his feet, stepping toward Vince. Turf shoes. They stopped and stood directly in front of Vince's flip-flops. "It was my fault," the feet said. "Take it easy on Lucas. It's cool."

My head snapped up. *Derek!*

I felt the panic spark up in me like a struck match. I shot my eyes around in all directions, searching for an escape. There was none. Was I breathing? How could he be here now? This was humiliating!

But he was here, Derek Griffin, now toe to toe with Vince, arms raised defensively. "It wasn't Lucas's fault. Okay?"

Vince took a moment to stare back at Derek. Then, flustered, he stomped back to his car. "This car was cherry!" He spat again and climbed into his driver's seat.

I dropped my head and turned to get back in my car. But before I could reach the handle, Derek's hand was on my shoulder. "Sorry, man. This is totally my fault. I stalled; just got my license, you know. I almost never drove in New York."

I smiled weakly. "It's no big deal."

"Well, I'm sure my insurance will pay for it," he said. "Anyway, you okay?" he asked.

I looked up at Derek from underneath my baseball cap. His eyes, fixed on mine, were green, groggy, bloodshot, beautiful. He put his other hand on my other shoulder, pressing on it, holding me just like he'd held Julian on the field yesterday. I could feel the warmth pulsing from his hands through my T-shirt. I savored it.

"Yeah, I'm cool," I mumbled. My mouth was moving one way, my brain the other. "No big deal."

"Forget about Vince," said Derek. "He's full of it, okay?"

"Except I am what he said I am," I spat. "I'm *gay*." I pulled my hoodie over my Mets cap. "Okay?" I squirmed out of his grasp.

There. I'd told him. He knew. I was ready for the worst.

But Derek just cocked his head back, wiping his hand across his face. "Okay, you're gay! But say it, dude, don't spray it!"

I looked at him, face screwed up. He smiled, just barely. Omigod, I'd just spat all over him. I lowered my eyebrows. He raised his. I turned to the side, wiping my mouth. He started to laugh.

"Sorry," I said, working hard to force a smile.

"Hey, man," he said. "It's cool." He pulled down on the strings of my hoodie, closing it over my face. "I'm on your side, okay?"

I blinked and paused in that blink, because for an instant, when my eyes were closed, I saw Derek, cupping my face in his hands, leaning forward to kiss me, tenderly, quietly. But when my eyes opened again, he was already two paces away.

"Okay," I breathed, watching him stride confidently to his car, turf shoes turning inward, pigeon-toed and athletic.

"See you next week!" he shouted when he reached his car.

I'm on your side.

6.

Sunday

"Ay, it is so dead tonight," said Sonja, looking through the window in the swinging kitchen door at the nearly empty Boca Mexicana dining room. "This is worse than that tailgater Friday."

"At least you can get some decent food around here, though," I said, swiping a chip and some CCQ off the tray she was holding.

"Quit it!" she hissed, slapping my hand away. "That's table four's!"

"Yum," I said as I opened the door for Sonja. "You better deliver it before I do that again."

Sonja rolled her eyes at me and flipped her hair. "Just like your mother's," said El Jefe, pointing at the photo above the stove. As a restaurant worker, by law Sonja should have her hair pulled back or something. But El Jefe didn't care. Tonight her hair was wild, curly, and spectacular. It entered the room well before she did and lingered for a spell after she left. "I'm going home. Gabriel will stay and cook tonight." El Jefe pulled the bandanna off his head and stuffed it in his back pocket. "I'm too tired."

"Good night, Papa," said Sonja, hugging him.

"Put on a sweater," said El Jefe. "That tank top is too skimpy." He kissed her forehead and walked out.

Sonja didn't even bother trying to hide her eye roll.

Sonja and I were the only two waitstaff on duty. At eight, when there were only two tables seated, Cate had gone home to chill out. She said she'd had a headache ever since Friday, when she drank a total of two rum and Cokes and three beers but didn't exchange numbers or kisses or anything, really, with Derek. Their extended chitchat about soccer was as far as they'd gotten.

I watched Sonja slip through the door, grab a water jug from the wait station, and slide the chips and CCQ onto table four, right in front of the windows that looked out into the parking lot. Sonja stepped around each of the four short-skirted women seated around the table, reaching over to fill their water glasses. With a "Your entrées should be out in a moment," she was back behind the kitchen door, tray hanging at her side.

"They think they're on *Sex and the City*," said Sonja.

"How '02," I said, rolling my eyes exaggeratedly.

After the Burger King incident, I'd stayed home pretty much all weekend, watching TV and enjoying the fact that Mom was in Santa Fe for the weekend visiting my aunt Carla. They had some kind of pact to see each other every other month or something. This weekend, it was Mom's turn to drive to New Mexico. So I had the place to myself and made the most of it, eating junk food and not showering. I spent a lot of time trying to figure out what to do next to hook up Cate with Derek. It was only a matter of time before they sealed the deal. After all, Derek would definitely like her. Cate was wonderful—she was smart, fun, funny. Plus she was totally beautiful. Any guy would be lucky to have her.

And Derek . . . Well, Derek was perfect.

Once they got together, once he was officially Cate's and I saw how happy they made each other, he would definitely be out from under my skin. Definitely. I also spent a lot of time trying not to think about what Derek had meant when he said, *I'm on your side.*

"Are you okay?" asked Sonja. "You don't look like yourself."

"I'm fine," I said, stifling a yawn. "I'm good." I ran my hands through my hair. "Just tired."

"So, I'm going to give Mike one more shot," said Sonja, strutting over to the prep area to check on table four's entrées. "But that's it."

"Fair enough," I replied. "But I am telling you, you're missing out on some prime action with Alex Norita."

"You *think*?" She stacked her tray with two burritos El Jefe, one camarones al diavolo, and one taquito appetizer and stepped toward the swinging door. "Open the door for me, *mijo*?"

I followed Sonja out to the floor, where Selena was just getting started with *"No me queda mas,"* a perfect, longing, woe-is-me breakup song. Sonja did a spin on her way to table four, almost dropping her taquitos. We both laughed.

"Mwah," I kissed.

Just then, a man, handsome, older, maybe in his forties, came in, talking on his cell phone. One look at his suit—dark gray, pin-striped—and I could tell he wasn't from Denver. People in Denver *never* wore suits, especially on Sunday night at a Mexican restaurant on Hampden Avenue. I walked to the front to greet him. He was talking fast.

"Forget the Singapore revenue stream. I'm talking about the Kuala Lumpur revenue. What? I can't hear you—hold on." He looked up at me and held up two fingers. "Table for two." Then, back into his cell phone, "Is Cavett there? Let me talk to Cavett." Then, back at me, "My son is parking the car."

On a busy night this would have annoyed me. Tonight, I just found it amusing. Grabbing two menus from the pile, I led Mr. Phone into the dining room. He pointed at table eleven, the booth behind the wait station. "Can we sit there?" he asked.

"Of course," I said, doing my best waiter.

I had just delivered glasses of water and a basket of chips for Mr. Phone, along with two salsas (red and green), when I heard the front door open. Mr. Phone waved. "Over here!"

I looked up. There was Derek, walking through the door, dirty-blond hair flopping in his face. I could see his eyes sparkling even from all the way across the restaurant. He was wearing a deep green T-shirt that stretched around his arms, but not too tight. Photo-printed on the front was a familiar old black-and-white picture of a man and woman kissing in Paris or someplace.

I sucked in my breath, hard, and felt my stomach seize up.

He pointed at me and walked over. "There he is," he said, crooked smiling. "I've been thinking about you." He punched me playfully on the shoulder. "How's your car?"

"Hi," I said. "It's fine, fine." *He'd been thinking about me?* I punched him back.

"Cate told me you worked here," he said. "She told me I had to get the CIA or the CMT or something. She said it's amazing."

"CCQ," I said calmly. "It's really good. I'll bring some."

"Hi, Dad," said Derek to Mr. Phone. Mr. Phone just waved back and kept talking to Kuala Lumpur or whoever. Derek looked back at me and shrugged. "He's in the resorts business, just dropping into town after stops in Aspen and Taos. We were supposed to go see the new *Revenge of the Dead* movie together, but his plane was late."

"*Revenge of the Dead*? Are we on part five now, or what?"

"Close. Part four. In the last one, the zombies managed to eat all the cab drivers in New York. Dad loves those movies. But whatever. He has another plane to catch at eleven, a red-eye to Brazil or the Canary Islands or something."

I smiled back, holding his gaze for a moment. His eyes were greener today, and was I imagining it, or were they tinged with just the tiniest bit of sadness? *How could he do that to you? How could anyone?* The mirror next to him cast candlelight across his profile, lighting up the hollow just under his Adam's apple. It pulsed slowly, hypnotizing me.

"Can I have some water, too?" he asked.

Snap out of it! I thought. I knew I had to get Cate over here, quick.

I looked over at Sonja, who was staring from behind the window in the swinging door, eyes wide. I practically knocked her down when I swung through to the kitchen.

"You might want to wipe the drool off your chin."

"I don't know what you're talking about," I said. I felt myself blush. "We've got to get Cate over here. It's too perfect. Hand me that phone," I said, pointing at the cordless manager's phone on the desk at the back.

I dialed Cate's number while Sonja fluffed her hair. *Come on, Catie. Answer.*

"Hello?" said Cate.

Whew. "Cate, we're swamped," I lied, relieved. "Can you come back in, please? Just to get us through this rush? Sonja and I are about to lose it." I grabbed a tub of bused dishes and shook it around to make restaurant sounds. I pointed at Sonja. She smiled and started banging some dishes. "CCQ!" I yelled. "Table eleven is hungry!"

"I was just about to eat dinner," said Cate. "And I haven't showered all day."

"Okay," I said. "But . . ." I picked up a saucer and

dropped it to the ground. It smashed with a back-of-the-restaurant *clang*. Sonja screamed, for real.

"Careful!" I yelled. "Cleanup!"

Sonja bared her teeth at me. "Hey, *loca*!" She pushed me out of the way. "Don't be breaking things."

"Crap," I muttered frantically into the phone. "Cate, I have to go. But we really need you down here."

I hung up.

"Did you have to break the plate?" said Sonja, grabbing for the broom. "You better be happy El Jefe's not here. You are seriously crazy."

"Gimme that. I'll clean it up." I held out my hand for the broom. "You have to admit, though, the sound effect was good." *Hurry up, Cate.*

I was sweating for the entire ten minutes it took Cate to arrive. She finally got there right after Derek's dad had gone to the parking lot for better reception, and Derek had asked for another bowl of CCQ and an order of enchiladas verdes. Cate slammed her way into La Boca's back door, red-faced and breathless. She was frantically trying to tie her hair back with a rubber band. "Okay!" she said, pushing up the sleeves of her baseball shirt. "I'm here. Where should I start?"

I handed her a bowl of CCQ and a basket of chips. "Table eleven," I said. "You're a real lifesaver."

"You owe me." She sighed, fake smiling on the way through the swinging door.

Sonja and I jumped to the window on the door to watch. It took Cate about five steps into the dining room before she stopped and looked around. Besides the *Sex and the City* table having another round of frozen margaritas, the only person in the restaurant was sitting alone at table eleven. Derek.

We were behind her, but we saw her shoulders drop, her neck droop, and her head shake. She inhaled deeply and turned back toward the kitchen. She glared at us in the window.

"Hey!" yelled Derek from his table, having spotted Cate's reflection in the mirror. "Is that my CCQ?"

"I think it is," said Cate, glare-smiling as she turned back around to take it to his table. "Here you go." She slid the CCQ in front of Derek.

"Hey, Cate," said Derek. He half stood up, smiling. I wondered if he would have stood up for me. I closed my eyes hard and tried to shake the thought out of my head. Of course he wouldn't have.

"Hi, Derek," said Cate, now at full waitress smile. "Sit. I'll be right back, okay?"

Cate strolled back toward the kitchen, running her tongue over her teeth, staring at us the whole way. Her tray hung at her side in one hand, while the other hand drew a finger across her throat. Sonja and I bumped fists in victory.

"Okay, now you *really* owe me," she whispered loudly after swinging into the back, brandishing her tray like a weapon. "Really crowded, huh? I look like crap! I'm *so* out of here!" She started untying her apron.

"If I'd told you, you wouldn't have come," I said, taking her hands. "But now that you're here . . ."

"Now that I'm here, I'm leaving! I look awful! And my head hurts. And he's here. And I'm just not ready for it." She looked over at Sonja. "Help me out."

Sonja shrugged and walked over to Cate. "I don't know, *mija*. I admit that Lucas is crazy, but I think you should stay. I mean, Derek's here, alone. You're here, alone. Neither one of you has eaten dinner. And PS, you look totally cute." Sonja reached over to remove the elastic holding Cate's ponytail. "Shake it out."

Cate pushed Sonja away and ran her fingers through her hair. "I like his T-shirt. That's a Cartier-Bresson photograph." She blew up at her bangs and peered out the swinging-door window. "He's alone?"

"Not exactly," I said. "But pretty much, yeah. Trust me."

"Okay," said Cate. "I *will* eat with him. But only because I haven't eaten yet." She took off her apron. "And because he looks lonely."

"Not that lonely," muttered Sonja, stepping on my toe.

I pushed Cate back out through the swinging door into the restaurant. I knew she was probably squirming a little, but this was good for her. She'd thank me. "Cate's shift just ended," I said.

"Does that mean you're leaving?" asked Derek.

Cate started to say, "Yes," but I cut her off. "Weren't you just saying you could go for an order of enchiladas verdes, Cate?" I led her to Derek's table. "I was just about to bring some for Derek."

"Are they good?" asked Derek, grinning at Cate.

Cate, trapped, smiled. "Yup," she clipped. "They are good."

"Can't wait," said Derek.

I pushed Cate down into the booth opposite Derek.

"I like your T-shirt," she said, voice cracking. "Cartier-Bresson."

"Thanks!" he said. "Are you into photography? I wish I knew how to take pictures like this." He looked down at his chest. "Wait a minute, it's upside down!" he joked.

Cate laughed, her eyes sparkling. *Easy, Cate. It wasn't that funny.*

With a "Be right back," I raced back to the kitchen, where I asked Gabriel to add another enchiladas verdes to the order. "For Cate!" I told him.

I was in the zone now, thinking only about Cate and Derek's impromptu date out in the dining room. I needed this to work, now. "Sonja," I barked, motioning her over, "listen. We cannot let her leave here without making another date with him."

"I don't know, Lucas. Is she even into this?" asked Sonja, peering out through the window in the door to see Cate sipping water and Derek dipping a chip. "I mean, look. They're not even really talking."

"They're not talking *because* they like each other," I said. "It's called being nervous. He's perfect for her and it's going to happen." When I said it out loud, I realized just how determined I really was. "Don't you want to see Cate happy? Do me this favor and I will get you a date with Mike Maccabee. Now here's what I want you to do."

Five minutes later, with Selena chirping through "*El Chico del Apartamento Cinco-doce,*" Sonja gathered up two orders of enchiladas verdes from under the heat lamp. I held open the door and followed her into the dining room, ducking behind the wait station, Derek's back to me. I watched her dance-walk over to table eleven, doing the washing machine, hair bouncing, singing along with Selena, *"El, sóló el . . ."*

"Dos enchiladas verdes!" she announced, filling the otherwise empty restaurant with her voice. She crossed to their table, shimmying, and laid down the two plates.

"Yum," said Derek, grabbing his fork excitedly. "I'm starving."

"Thank you, Sonja." Cate smiled at Sonja, lips pursed. "Where's Lucas?" she asked suspiciously.

"Listen, Cate," said Sonja, ignoring her question. "Don't make plans for Friday, *chica*. I want to see that new *Revenge of the Dead* movie."

"I'm sorry, what?"

"Yeah. *Revenge of the Dead*. The zombie one."

"No way!" said Derek, looking at Cate. "It's supposed to be awesome."

"Do you like horror movies?" asked Sonja, turning to Derek with a her hand on her hip. Derek nodded like a little boy, hair flopping. "Maybe you should join us," said Sonja. "Don't you think he should join us, Cate?"

Cate looked back at the wait station, where I was rearranging the already-rearranged hot sauce rack, then back at Sonja. "*Revenge of the Dead?*" she asked.

"Yes," said Sonja. "So, Derek, are you in?"

Nice, Cindy Subtlety, I thought.

"I don't know. Are you going, Lucas?" asked Derek, who'd craned around and was now staring at me.

"I'm sorry," I said, turning around, clearing my throat, and trying to sound nonchalant. "What? I wasn't paying attention. I was, um, folding napkins."

"Are you going to the movies on Friday?" he asked. "With these guys?" He motioned at Cate and Sonja. "*Revenge of the Dead?*"

"Um, yeah," I mumbled. I felt an ache in my chest. "I guess." I dropped a handful of napkins. "Oops," I said.

"Then count me in," said Derek, smiling at Cate.

"*Revenge of the Dead?*" Cate asked again, staring at Sonja.

"That's the one," said Sonja. "Friday."

"Friday it is, then," said Derek. "I'm scared already."

Sonja raised her eyebrow at me. "Aren't we all?"

7.

Wednesday

"SO, CATE, DO YOU LIKE HIM OR WHAT?"

It was the third day of the new school year, lunchtime. Sonja, Cate, and I were on the front lawn. Sonja was trying to organize all the paper she'd accumulated since classes started on Monday, shuffling revised schedules, reading lists, and overdue registration forms. "What is all this junk?" She sighed. "What am I supposed to do with this?"

"Just sign El Jefe's name," I said.

"Lucas!" snapped Cate, gasping dramatically. "I'm shocked."

"It's called do-it-yourself parenting," I said. "Last I checked, the three of us were pros at it."

The lawn was crowded with students milling, chatting, gossiping, groping, flirting, yelling, rushing, and lying around.

Across the lawn I could see Derek and Julian kicking a hacky sack back and forth in the sun.

"Well? Do you like him?" I asked Cate again, for the third time since lunch began.

"I barely know him!" she protested. "Sonja, make him stop."

Sonja popped open a soda. "The first Diet Coke of the day," she said, holding up her can in a toast. "Fabulous." She had a sip and began opening an official-looking envelope. "So, Cate, do you like him?"

"Shut up!" Cate was clearly exasperated. She turned away from Sonja and me, watching Derek and Julian hacky sacking.

Derek leaped for the sack, his red Welcome to New York, Now Duck! T-shirt riding up to expose his lower back. For a moment he froze, and I was mesmerized by the little dimple above his tailbone. He missed the hacky and rolled onto the ground, sprawling, laughing, legs flying. I forced myself to look away.

"Hey, Julian!" Cate waved.

Julian waved back.

"He's so cute," said Cate. "I love him."

"Who, Derek?" I teased.

"No! Julian!" she protested.

"So why are you blushing?"

"I am not!" protested Cate, but I knew that she knew that she was. "Okay, fine," she said, adjusting her sunglasses. "Fine, I admit it, he's cute."

Sonja looked up from her papers in approval. "I heard that," she said.

"And?" I prodded.

"And he's funny," she said. "And he's nice to Julian. And that's it."

"Good enough for now," I said.

"Um, Lucas?" asked Sonja, holding up the official-looking letter. "Um, Cate? Um, you guys? Can you take a look at this?" She handed her letter to me. "It's from the vice principal. I don't get it."

"Let me see that," I said, grabbing the letter.

"I think it's bad," said Sonja.

I read aloud. "*Sonja Perez, room 42*, blah blah. *We are required by state statute number 443/33/209b to inform you that you must fulfill two required credits to remain on track for graduation in spring 2006. Your missing credits are listed below.* Blah blah, okay, here: *Biology, one credit*." I stopped reading. "What's the big deal, Sonja? You can do biology if you need to. Just drop music appreciation and take bio. Who cares?"

"Keep reading," she said, grabbing Cate's arm with two hands. "Oh, God."

"*Physical education, one credit.*" I stopped reading. "Oh," I said. "I see the problem."

"What's the problem?" asked Cate. "Just take PE!" She looked over at Sonja. "What's the big deal?"

Sonja looked at Cate like she was speaking in tongues. "Oh God," mumbled Sonja, turning to me. "Oh God. Lucas, what am I going to do?"

Cate rolled her eyes. "You have to get over this PE thing, Sonja," she said. "Just suck it up and do it. It's not worth risking your graduation over."

"That's easy for you to say, Miss Jock, Lifeguard, Triathlete, *whatever*. I do not *run* in front of people. Okay?" She buried her head in Cate's shoulder. "I'm not doing it. I just won't graduate. It doesn't matter, if I'm going to take over the restaurant anyway."

Cate put her arm around Sonja. "Don't be a complete moron."

I took Sonja's hand. "Don't worry, Sonja. You're graduating. Let's go to the VP's office and see what we can work out."

"Really?" whimpered Sonja. She shook loose from Cate's grasp and put her hands in mine.

I kissed Cate on the cheek. "Cate, see you later." I put my free arm around Sonja. "Come on, baby," I coaxed, guiding her into the crowd.

I led Sonja into the building. After negotiating our way through two hallway scuffles and a crew of post–pep rally drill teamers, we rounded the corner to the administration "wing," where the principal, vice principal, nurse, college counselor, and other school officials spent their days, safely sealed off from the student body. Three bored-looking students were waiting on a bench across from the chest-high reception desk, behind which buzzed three big-haired office assistants. Beyond them, closed doors marked the domains of the senior administration.

At the main desk, filling out a small pink form, was Lueree, one of the senior office assistants. "Hi, Lucas," she said from behind several inches of makeup, including . . . Were those fake eyelashes? "Did you have a good summer?"

"Nice highlights!" I said brightly, hoping her hair was, in fact, lighter.

"Thank you!" she said, taking off her glasses, which hung from her neck, and fluttering her eyes. "You're sweet," she said. Lueree had loved me ever since my sophomore year, when I'd tried to set her up with the cute guy who picked up the school's recycling. Unfortunately he hadn't been interested, so I'd lied and told Lueree he'd said he was just getting over a horrible breakup and couldn't get involved with anyone for a long time, especially someone as beautiful as Lueree, who could easily break his heart. "What can I do for you, Lucas?"

"I'm here to help my girlfriend Sonja straighten some things out with her schedule," I said.

"Oh. Hi, Sonja. I didn't see you there," said Lueree, her face dropping. She'd seen Sonja in here before, more than once, and not always for the best reasons.

"Hi," said Sonja, looking at the ground. I kicked her from behind the counter, where Lueree couldn't see. "Your hair looks really pretty," she said, barely looking up.

"Hmm," sniffed Lueree.

I handed Lueree the letter. "According to this note, it seems that Sonja is a couple of credits behind for graduation. She'd like to make those credits up."

"So I see," said Lueree, pushing on her glasses and scanning the letter. She turned back to her computer and started typing. "Let's see. *P-e-r-e-z* . . . Okay, Sonja, I can switch you into biology, but you'll have to drop music appreciation."

Sonja groaned.

"That's great," I said. "Thanks, Lueree."

"And I can put you into eighth-period PE."

Sonja groaned again, much louder.

"Actually, Lueree," I said. "That might be a problem. Sonja's made an ambitious decision to pursue trigonometry during eighth period." I winked at Sonja. "Is there any other PE opening?"

"Nope," said Lueree, dropping her glasses. "All booked till summer school." Behind her, the standard-issue school wall clock ticked forward one minute with a frighteningly loud *click*.

"Is that our only option?" I asked. "Trig is more important than PE, don't you think? By the way, that scent you're wearing is great." I was laying it on thick, but I knew Lueree would love it.

"You like?" She held out her wrist for me to sniff.

"Yummy," I said.

"Hmm," said Lueree, turning back to her computer. "Well, there's one other option. Erika Abritz has been, um, *retired* as manager of the boys' varsity soccer team."

"Really?" I said, leaning in. I knew Lueree loved to gossip on the down low. "What happened? Do tell." I couldn't have cared less.

"You didn't hear it here," said Lueree, looking around and lowering her voice. "But she was caught distributing, um, favors of a personal nature to one of the team members."

"*No!*" I gasped. "And what happened to the player she was, um, favoring?" I wondered if it was Vince.

Lueree pursed her lips. "Punish a member of a winning

sports team? At this school?" She swatted air with her hand. "Not a chance."

I nodded and winked. "I hear ya, Lueree. Tsk."

Lueree went on, speaking to me, not Sonja. "So, Sonja could assume the job as soccer team manager, for which she would earn one PE credit. It's approximately two to three hours a day, assisting the team at practices and games, home and away. It involves making sure the equipment is in good order, setting up the benches, managing the schedule, taking notes at all team meetings, and clearing the locker room of dirty towels. It will also involve traveling, including a weekend in Pueblo for the state round-robin tournament in a couple of weeks. The job starts next Monday."

It sounded terrible.

"She'll take it," I said.

Sonja glared at me. "What? I don't think so. I don't carry clipboards, I don't wear a whistle, and I definitely don't pick up sweaty old soccer player towels. The answer is no. I can't!"

"So I'll just put you down for summer school, then," said Lueree coldly.

"No!" I yelled. "I mean, no thank you, Lueree. Give us one second." I turned to Sonja. "Take this, Sonja. Trust me, it's better than PE. And definitely better than PE in the summer. Just suck it up and do it. Besides, it'll look great on your applications."

"What applications?" asked Sonja, grabbing a lock of hair to twirl.

"College applications, you dope!" I snapped at Sonja.

"You'll get the credit, and you won't have to exercise. At all." She looked at the ground.

"I hate you," she said.

"Just think, Sonja: Guys in towels." I said it before I thought about it and immediately an image of Derek, showered, in a towel, burst into my head. *I'm on your side,* he was saying. *I've been thinking about you.* "I almost wish I could take the job!" I half joked, winking at Lueree.

"Wait," said Sonja, snapping her gum. "If it's so great, why don't you do it with me?"

"Even if I wanted to," I said, "there's only one soccer manager."

"Actually," said Lueree, looking at her computer screen, "according to this e-mail, it looks like Coach Le Beouf has asked for two managers this year. I guess the team is bigger than ever. So, Lucas, if you wanted to . . ."

I looked at Sonja. She looked at me. "Please?" she moaned. "Pleeeease? I swear I will love you forever. . . ." Sonja blinked her big brown eyes at me. "Please, best friend in the whole world?"

I smelled trouble. But I knew there was no way out of this. Sonja would never take no for an answer. This would be a good way for me to get closer to Derek. For the sake of hooking him up with Cate, of course.

The clocked ticked again, marking another moment I was caught up in. I turned to face Lueree. "We start on Monday?"

8.

Friday

"WHOSE IDEA WAS IT TO SEE THIS ZOMBIE MOVIE?" I ASKED the girls. It was raining pretty hard and we were on our way to meet Derek at the movie theater for our date. I mean Cate's date.

"You," said Sonja. "You chose it. Remember?" She snapped her gum, eyeing me in the rearview mirror. "I can't even believe I'm here. I don't even have a date," she whined.

"I'm your date," I said. "But I'm not putting out later, so don't get all excited."

"My point exactly." Sonja scowled.

"I think out of all the monsters," offered Cate from the backseat. "I like zombies best."

"I like mummies," said Sonja.

"Vampires," I said. "I like vampires."

"Hot," said Sonja.

"I know," I said. "That neck-biting thing. So hot."

"No," said Sonja, hitting me on the shoulder. "I mean

hot." She pointed at the theater entrance, underneath the huge marquee. There was Derek, squinting around at the crowd, in those faded jeans and a just barely wet T-shirt with a photo-print of Andy Warhol on the front.

"Wow," said Cate, blushing. "Andy Warhol. That's a famous photograph of him. I can't remember who took it."

"Wow," said Sonja. "Nice pecs."

"Hands off, Sonja," I said sternly. "Remember why we're here!"

"Take it easy," said Cate. "This is not a date. It's all of us together."

"If you say so," said Sonja.

We parked, hopped out of the Subaru, and sprinted through the rain to the entrance. Sheltered from the rain by the massive marquee, the entrance was teeming with kids in baggy clothes and trucker hats.

Derek waved us down. "I got tickets!" he said. "It was almost sold out, so I just bought four. We're in."

"No way!" said Sonja, holding out her hand. "Thanks!"

"Here's a ten," I said, fishing in my back pocket. "Thanks, man."

"Nope, it's on me," said Derek, pushing my hand away.

"No," said Cate, pulling out her debit card. "Just let me get some cash and I'll pay you back."

"Forget it," said Derek, putting one arm around Cate, the other around me. "It's my treat."

"Does that include snacks?" asked Sonja, pushing her way through the overcrowded revolving door entrance, knocking a couple of baggy-jeaned boys out of her way.

"'Cause I need popcorn. A large one. And a huge-ass Diet Coke. Omigod, Lucas, don't look. It's Alex Norita."

"Don't mind Sonja," I said to Derek. I jumped into a revolving door slot with him, leaving Cate behind. "I'll get the snacks. What do you want?" I shuffled behind him awkwardly.

"Nothing, man, thanks. I'm good," said Derek, stepping free from the door. "But what about Cate?"

"Me too," said Cate, emerging from the door behind us. "I mean, me either. I mean, nothing for me." She smiled at Derek. "Andy Warhol." She pointed at his T-shirt.

"It's a self-portrait," he said, winking. "Or so he claimed."

"I hardly know anything about him," said Cate.

"There were a lot of mysterious things about Andy Warhol," said Derek. "Wouldn't you say so, Lucas?" He bent down and butted me in the chest with his head.

"Are you sure you don't want any snacks?" I asked, backing up, flustered. "They're on me."

Sonja looked back and grabbed at me, pinching my arm. "Lucas!" She pursed her lips.

I drew a sharp breath, wondering what she meant. Did she mean that I was acting like it was *my* date and not Cate's? Was that what she meant? Probably, since that's what I was doing. I felt a sharp stab of guilt deep in my gut.

I took a step to the side. "Listen," I choked, leaning over to Cate. "The theater's filling up. Go with Derek and find seats." I winked at her.

"But . . ." she said.

"Derek, find seats," I said. "Take Cate."

"Okay," said Derek. "After you." He gestured to Cate, pointing her through the crowd and into the theater. "Have you ever seen any of Warhol's movies with Joe Dalessandro? I went to a retrospective once ..."

Sonja and I hit the snacks line.

"Um," said Sonja, "is that a pickle in your pocket?"

"What do you mean?" I said, sounding more pathetic than innocent.

"*Ay*, please," said Sonja. "It's called a crush, Lucas. I've seen it before."

"Okay, Debbie Drama," I said. "Give me a break! It's not like I'm trying to *get* him or anything. I know why we're here. We're here for Catie, who totally deserves someone as amazing as Derek. Besides," I said. "He's not even gay." *I don't think.*

"He's not?" asked Sonja, mockingly. "Are you sure? The guy only has hands for you."

"He's just touchy-feely, that's all," I said. "He does that to everyone."

"Whatever," she said. "Goobers or Raisinets?"

We'd just ordered when someone grabbed at my waist, sharply pinching my sides just above my hips. I turned around to see Derek standing there with a disappointed look.

"We couldn't find four seats together. Cate is back in the theater saving two up front, and I think there are a couple of spots in the back if we get some people to move. Sonja, do you want to go sit with Cate and I'll find other seats with Lucas?"

Sonja arched her left eyebrow.

"No!" I said sharply. "Derek, you should go sit with Cate!"

"Are you sure?"

"Definitely," I said. "Go." I could feel Sonja watching me.

"Okay, man," said Derek. "I can deal, but next time . . ." He poked two fingers into my side. It tickled. "Have fun!" He trotted back into the movies.

"Check out that ass," said Sonja.

"Shut up, Sonja," I said.

The girl behind the counter handed us our snacks. Popcorn, Goobers, *and* Raisinets. And two massive Diet Cokes. "That's $14.75, please."

I reached into my back pocket and pulled out a ten. I reached again for more. Nothing. I patted down my pockets. "Damn!" I snapped.

"What?" asked Sonja.

"I don't have enough," I said. "I thought I had another ten. Do you have any cash?"

"Nope," she said. "I don't even have my ATM card!"

"Fourteen seventy-five, please. People are waiting!"

"I'm sorry," I said. "We have to give back the Goobers."

"Not the Goobers!" said Sonja. "Give back the Raisinets!"

"I can't go back," said the girl. "I have to ring it over again."

"*Ay,*" said Sonja.

"Here, Sonja," came a tinny voice from behind us. "Let

me." It was Alex Norita, standing behind us with a couple of other *Star Wars* club guys. He held out a five-dollar bill.

"No way," I said. "Thanks anyway, Alex, we couldn't."

"Thank you, Alex," said Sonja. She grabbed the five from Alex and handed it to the girl. "That's very kind of you. Lucas will pay you back on Monday."

Alex smiled broadly. "Are you seeing *Revenge of the Dead*?" he asked. "That's what we're here for. Maybe we could all sit together!"

"No," lied Sonja. "We're seeing the new Mandy Moore movie."

"Well," said Alex, "have fun. Maybe we'll get out at the same time and we'll see each other again."

"Maybe," said Sonja, smiling stiffly.

"You look great, Sonja," said Alex. "Like Selena. Do you know Selena Quintanilla, *la reina*?"

Sonja froze. "Selena? What do you know about Selena?"

"I'm from Texas," said Alex. "Corpus Christi. *Me gusta a Selena.*"

"I thought you were Japanese," said Sonja suspiciously.

"I *am* Japanese. From Corpus Christi. And everyone knows Selena in Corpus Christi. Anyway, I always thought you looked like her," he said. "But better."

Sonja turned to me and crossed her eyes. "See you later, Alex," she said politely.

"*Si una vez,*" he replied as we walked away. He turned back to his friends.

"*Si una vez?*" I asked. "What's that mean? 'One time'?"

"It's a Selena song," said Sonja. "About taking chances. I can't believe he just did that in front of all his friends. What kind of guy hits on a girl in front of his friends?"

"A gutsy one," I said, impressed by Alex's honesty and fearlessness. "So, Mandy Moore, huh?" I asked Sonja, who was cradling a bucket of popcorn like a baby.

"I'm sorry. I lied. I mean, he's nice and all, but . . ." She sighed. "I didn't want to sit with him."

"Car?" I asked.

"Perfect."

Cate could definitely get a ride home from Derek. We left a voice message on her cell, which we knew she'd turned off, and raced back to the car, arms full of goodies.

These were my favorite times with Sonja, just cruising, singing along to endless, mindless pop music. Sonja squealed when a Selena song came on.

"I love this! *I could fall in looooooooove* . . . This is one of her rare English songs!"

"I wonder if the movie's any good," I said, reading street signs through the rainy windshield. University, York, Gaylord. We were getting closer to home.

"I don't," said Sonja, checking her teeth in the passenger mirror. "I don't care."

"I wonder if Cate and Derek are scared," I said. "Do you think they're holding hands?"

Sonja didn't answer. She was humming along to Selena.

"I hope so," I said. "That's the plan, after all. Do you think they'll hook up tonight? It's their first good chance."

"The sooner, the better," said Sonja, turning up the radio.

Moments later, I spotted Hampden Avenue, just a block from Sonja's.

"So," I asked. "Are you ready for your new job with the team? I really have no idea what to expect. I mean, I know what we're supposed to be doing, but I have no idea what it's going to be like, you know?"

"Lucas," she said, covering her ears. "It's Friday. We have two more days to *not* think about that. Let's enjoy them."

She was right again. I dropped her off with an air kiss. "Mwah. See you Sunday for work."

"Thanks for reminding me, Brady Bummer!"

I cocked my eyebrow. "Are you making fun of me?"

I drove home, backing into the carport, happy to be out of the rain. Sliding open the glass door that led from the carport to the dark kitchen, I realized that once again I'd made it home before Mom. I should have known when she left for her date wearing strappy stilettos that she wouldn't be back before one in the morning. Good for her, I guess. I mean, at least someone's out there having a good time.

Was she having a good time? I could never tell.

I wandered back into my room. It's like a cave. No windows. No air. No light. Actually, before it was my room, it was probably a closet. I live in a closet. How ironic.

I hit the light switch, flooding the room with sharp overhead light. "Jesus," I said aloud. My room was a total mess. My twin bed was tucked along the far wall, covered in clothes, most of them things I'd tried on but didn't end up wearing. The cabinet next to my bed was a chaotic stack of CDs, books, magazines. Game Boy cartridges. Sneakers in piles. Two pairs of Rollerblades. A map of the world tacked onto the wall, lopsided. The bed wasn't made, but the plaid pillowcases didn't go with the striped sheets anyway.

I tossed my keys into the mess, knowing it would be a pain to find them tomorrow. I closed the door behind me, put on a Dido CD, and sipped my soda.

I stripped to my boxers and surveyed myself in the full-length mirror that was screwed into the back of my door. I sucked in my gut, which made my ribs stick out. I turned the other way, sticking out my butt. I flexed my biceps. My shoulders drooped.

I needed to start lifting weights or something. I hung a blue batik cloth from Pier 1 over the mirror and turned off the overhead light. I switched on my bedside lamp.

Without Sonja to distract me, Derek was now right smack in the front of my mind. *Damn it!* I lay down on my bed and closed my eyes, confused. I loved Cate and wanted her to be happy. And maybe Derek could help make her happy. Besides, I *knew* there was no chance I'd ever be with Derek. It wasn't even worth considering. So why couldn't I squash this crush?

I wondered if Derek and Cate were getting along. I wondered if they liked the movie. I wondered if they'd kissed. I wondered if they were kissing right now. I wondered what Derek kissed like. I wondered if he was better than Marcus. I wondered what he looked like with no shirt on.

I pictured him running, tapping the ball in front of him with his legs, those legs, powering him forward. Derek's legs, which led to Derek's shorts, which covered Derek.

Opening my eyes, I reached over to turn out the light. I'm not sure when I fell asleep, but I know what I was thinking about when I did.

9.

Monday

"THIS SUCKS," SAID SONJA FOR ABOUT THE THIRTIETH TIME since we'd started our first session as soccer team managers a half hour before. "This is disgusting. Where have these towels been? They should give us rubber gloves. This sucks. This sucks." Her voice bounced hollowly off the tile walls and floor.

"Hey, Wendy Whiner," I said, tossing another towel into the gray laundry bin, "you can do better than, 'This sucks. This sucks.' Can you be a little more creative, please?" I pushed the squeaky-wheeled laundry bin around the corner into another row of lockers, eyes peeled for towels to toss in the bin or, better yet, stray jockstraps to ogle.

"You want creative?" she yelled from around the corner. "How about, 'This *blows*'? How's that?" Sonja was moving slowly, taking small steps, pausing frequently, and complaining loudly in the dank air. "Am I even legally allowed to be in here? I mean, it's the boys' locker room!"

"Oh, please," I said. "Like you've never been here before. I guess you'd rather spend next summer wearing gym shorts and running laps?" Sonja heaved herself around the corner with a groan. I held up my hand. "Save it," I shushed.

"Harsh, Lucas," mumbled Sonja, bending over to pick up a pair of jockey shorts. "Ew!"

"Believe me, I don't want to be here any more than you do. I'm only here for you."

She tossed the jockey shorts into the bin. "Why don't I believe that?"

I sucked in my breath. "Sonja, you're crazy." But she knew me too well.

At work last night, Cate had filled us in on what had happened after the movie on Friday: nothing. Not an invitation to grab some coffee. Not a long, slow drive home. Not even a peck on the cheek. Nothing. She didn't seem crushed, just vaguely disappointed. Even so, it made me want to reach out and give her a hug.

But at the same time, I couldn't help it: The whole thing made me curious. Was he just not that into her? Was she giving off the wrong signals? Were they both too shy? Too tired? Was he just not into girls?

I gasped when I thought it. *Impossible. He's not gay.* It was too much to imagine.

After work last night I'd stayed up late scouring soccer websites, trying to learn everything I'd ignored back in my days on the Kickapoo squad. I'd made a list of soccer positions and learned some basic configurations. I'd studied the names of star players. I had a lot to learn, but I wanted to be sure I could talk soccer, at least a little. With Derek or anyone.

I felt Sonja at my arm. "Sorry, *mijo*," she said, tenderly squeezing my shoulder. "I didn't mean anything by that. I'm just glad you're here, in this locker room, suffering through this with me." She looked into my eyes. "Thank you."

"Really?" I fished weakly.

"Yes," said Sonja, reading me perfectly. "I know you didn't have to be here. You're giving up every one of your afternoons for me, and I love you for it. Besides, I am going to need someone to bitch to at this job. And you're it."

"Don't mention it," I said. I turned to Sonja and held out my hands. "Purell me."

She dug through her shoulder bag and squirted me with her travel-sized sanitizer. "So, what gives with Cate and Derek, anyway? No action? Are you losing your touch or what?"

Was I? Or was I sabotaging myself? Was I missing something? What was it?

Before I could answer, the locker room doors burst open with a crash. Coach Le Beouf, TJ's biggest, loudest, hairiest sports coach, bellowed in, "Sondra! Luis! On the field!" The doors slammed shut again. "Now, please!"

Sonja turned to me. "Who's Sondra and Luis?"

"I think that's us," I said, sliding on my sunglasses. "Let's go."

We tossed the last of the towels into the bin and walked out through the gym and onto the field. We approached the sidelines, where Coach Le Beouf was pacing, watching the twenty members of the soccer team do drills. He was clapping, shouting, "Eyes on the ball, ladies!"

I looked for Derek and found him in a drill circle next to Julian, watching the ball intently. Twice the ball came to him, and twice he burst into action, kicking it back into play. The sound his foot made when it thwacked the ball was rich and full and solid—much more so than that of the other players, even Vince. Derek appeared to be years older than they were, steadier. He moved with a much clearer confidence.

"We're here, Coach Le Beouf," I said, trying not to notice the puddles of yellow sweat under his arms.

"What?" he barked, not looking at me. "Scrimmage, ladies!" he yelled. "Shirts and skins! I want 3-2-2-1 on 3-1-3-1. Griffin, you sweep for the skins!"

Griffin.

Half the players, including Derek, stripped off their shirts. Sonja lowered her sunglasses for a better look, focusing on Vince. "This is getting better by the minute," she said. She threaded the bottom hem of her T-shirt through the V-neck to expose her belly. "Shirts and skins. *Me gusta.*"

Vince whistled at her. Sonja scowled back, pretending to be annoyed. "Never let them know you like it," she said.

I swallowed and tried not to stare at Derek.

"Coach?" I said again.

"Set up the bench!" yelled Coach Le Beouf. "Here, on the sideline! It's back in the locker room! Also clean towels, Gatorade, shin pads, balls. Go!" He waved us away without even looking at us. "You two are going to need a lot of work to be ready for Pueblo." He turned his attention back to the field. "Sawyer! You're on skins!"

Sawyer. That was Julian. I looked over at him. He waved to me, reluctantly taking off his shirt.

Sonja cracked her knuckles. "Pueblo? What's he talking about?"

"That's the statewide round-robin tournament the week after next. It's in Pueblo. Remember? Lueree told us we'd have to go." I turned toward the gym.

"For a whole weekend?" she whined.

"Yes, Sonja. A whole weekend. Let's get the bench." I took her by the hand and walked her back to the gym.

We set up the bench, mixed up some powdered Gatorade, and sat down to watch the scrimmage. Derek, of course, was brilliant, stealing, passing, moving the ball with a skill well above all the other players'. Vince was the only other player who even came close. Watching Vince and Derek square off, stealing the ball from each other, racing against each other and clipping at the feet, was spellbinding. It was like watching a dance. I could almost see what Cate had seen in Vince.

Almost.

Sonja was equally brilliant, reclining and posing in the grass like that girl who truckers put on their mud flaps: back arched, breasts thrust forward, tummy sucked in, hair flowing behind her.

"Cate should be here to see this," I said. "She'd flip for him for sure."

"She's already flipped," said Sonja. "Can't you tell?"

I took my eyes off the game and stared at my shoes.

Just then, Coach Le Beouf exploded. "Score!" he yelled. "*Goooooooooaaaaallll!!* Nice work, DiSimone!" I realized he was talking to Vince. "Sawyer, you should have had that. Okay, ladies, gather around. Grab some Gatorade!"

The players came jogging over to the sidelines. Vince, who was on the shirts team but was now wearing his T-shirt on his head, was leading the way. Derek and Julian walked slower, behind the rest of the team.

"Hey, Lucas," said a couple of junior members of the team. "What's up?"

I nodded and smiled at them. "Hey!"

Soon nine or ten guys were clamoring around the two coolers, Sonja and I each filling cups with the syrupy drink. "Hey, boys," said Sonja. "Thirsty?" She held out a Dixie cup full of Gatorade. Several hands grabbed at it. "One at a time," she said, smiling. "Behave."

"Gatorade," said Vince, pushing his way to my cooler, glaring at me. "Manager."

I drew him a Dixie cup full of Gatorade and held it out to him. He grabbed it out of my hand, saying, "So, you're the manager, Lucas. Finally, you've found a way to get into the locker room." He turned to the line of team members. "Watch your jockstraps, boys!"

I dropped my eyes and continued drawing cups of Gatorade. I wanted to see how much support he had. Happily, Vince only got chuckles from two players. The rest of the team ignored him.

"That's enough, Vince," said Coach Le Beouf. "Linus is a crucial member of this team now. As is Sylvia. They are your managers and you need to respect them."

"Yeah, shut up, Vinnie," said Sonja, clearly staring at his abs. "You suck."

"Sonja," I hissed, shooting her a pleading look. "Don't." *You need this gig.*

"Actually, Sonja, I heard that you suck," taunted Vince. "I heard that's why you were hired to manage the boys' team. Free service for varsity members." Several guys laughed.

"Vin-dog," said Sonja, her finger wagging, "you wouldn't know what to do with it even if I *did* lay it out for you. Needledick."

"Vince," said Coach Le Beouf again, cutting her off. "Back off. Don't be a pain in my ass."

Sonja turned to me, exhaling. "I hate him," she said.

"I know," I said. "We all do."

Just then, Derek and Julian finally reached the bench. Unlike Vince, they'd both put their shirts back on.

"Hey, Lucas!" said Derek. "Hey, Sonja!" He high-fived her and punched my shoulder. "What's up, managers?"

"That's right," I said. "Managers. So watch your step." I playfully punched him back. Sonja kicked me from behind.

I gulped. *Checked.*

"Awesome!" said Derek, punching me again. He passed the soccer ball he'd been dribbling to my feet, where I toed it back and forth.

"Careful," said Vince. "Are you sure Lucas is ready for a soccer ball? We don't want to see him get hurt."

If Derek heard Vince, he didn't act like it. He just stared right at me. "Over here," he said. I passed it, right to his feet. He passed it back. I returned.

"Sawyer," barked Coach Le Beouf, summoning Julian. "Get over here. Explain that last miss to me. How could you not save that?"

"I'm sorry, Coach." Julian shook his head. "I guess I just lost concentration."

"No apologies, Sawyer," said Coach. "Walk with me." They stepped out into the field, Coach's arm around Julian's shoulders. I guess Sawyer, I mean *Julian*, needed some coaching. I knew that Coach Le Beouf put a lot of stock in Julian. He was a huge asset to the team.

Good thing Cate isn't here, I thought. She'd be following them around the field right now, trying to listen in.

I kicked the ball back to Derek, who stopped it, then took a step back and nailed the ball with a solid, powerful, satisfying *thwack* halfway across the field and into the unattended goal. He smiled. "I love that sound."

"More Gatorade?" asked Sonja.

"Yes, please," said Derek, holding out his cup to Sonja and smiling. He had a purple Gatorade mustache. I wanted to lick it off. "It's strange having a girl manager," he said, smirking. "I think I like it."

He's flirting with her! I thought. *In front of everyone! In front of me!* I needed to break this up. *What about Cate?*

"And how many touchdowns did you score today?" asked Sonja, flirting back. Vince scoffed somewhere behind me.

I grabbed the cup from Derek's outstretched hand. "They aren't called touchdowns," I said, filling Derek's cup while Sonja flipped her hair. "They're called field goals." I knew this wouldn't exactly impress Derek, but at least he and the rest of the team would know that I knew the basics about soccer. "Field goals," I said again, louder so I was sure everyone in earshot heard. I tapped the soccer ball with my toes.

"Just goals, Lucas," whispered Derek, leaning in. "They're not field goals, just goals." He smiled and winked, then slapped my butt, sending my shoulder blades back and stiffening my spine. "But you knew that."

I heard Vince snicker behind Derek. I strained to hear him say "homo" or something, but he didn't. Not this time. He didn't need to.

"Duh," I said, embarrassed and grinning like an idiot.

I took a swipe at the soccer ball with my right foot, hoping to kick it emphatically onto the field, making the sound that Derek made, to earn my way out of this moment. Only I missed. I grazed the ball with the side of my foot and sent it spinning wildly into the air. It came down on Vince's hand, knocking his Gatorade all over his bare chest.

"Dammit!" yelled Vince.

I cringed, head down, waiting for the reprisal that I knew must be coming. I waited for Vince to jump on me the way he had at the drive-through.

But all I heard was a chorus of players, snickering. I looked up, expecting to see fingers pointed in my direction. But the fingers were pointed at Vince. They weren't snickering at me. They were snickering at Vince, dripping with grape Gatorade. I collected high fives from four players.

It wasn't until then that I saw Cate up on the hill just beyond the soccer field, sitting cross-legged, facing the field. *Checking up on Julian,* I thought. I waved, but she didn't wave back. I guess she didn't see.

Sonja and I got back to work, picking up Dixie cups now and collecting the next set of dirty towels.

On the way home from practice, after dropping Sonja off, I stopped by the Barnes & Noble, where I found some lonely floor space in a back corner near the sports section. There, head bowed, as if I'd be tested tomorrow, I pored over a stack of soccer books and magazines, from *Soccer for Dummies* to a roster list of the biggest European teams. I wanted to know everything Derek knew. I wanted to feel what it was like inside his head. I memorized every offensive and defensive formation in the book and learned the names of key international players until they started turning off the lights.

10.

Tuesday

"SO WHAT'S UP, CATE?" ASKED SONJA, MOVING ASIDE A JAR OF olives to reach the last Diet Coke in Cate's cavernous refrigerator. "Has he made a move yet or what? It's been almost two weeks."

"What?" said Cate, shifting on her bar stool. "Who?"

"Derek!" snapped Sonja, looking at me, exasperated. "Who do you think?"

"Yeah, Misty Mysterious," I prodded. I started to rearrange a bowl of fruit on the counter, putting the apples at the bottom and the avocados at the top. "I happen to know you've walked home with him twice in the past two weeks, once stopping along the way for a coffee. You can't keep us in the dark. Make my day and tell me he's made a move."

"Give me a break, Lucas," said Cate, focused on her journal. "Besides, I thought you'd lost interest. You haven't asked me about him in over a week."

Was that true? Had it really been that long?

"So, guys, what gives?" Sonja said. "Cate and Derek should be fully bumping by now, but nothing's happening. Lucas?"

"Maybe Derek isn't like other guys," I said.

"What's that supposed to mean?" said Sonja, pulling her hair up off her neck and wrapping it into a bun on the top of her head.

"Maybe Derek's not like other guys," I explained, thinking fast as I went. "He's not like Vince, who can't wait to get his pants off with pretty much any girl, then tell everyone he knows. Maybe Derek is a gentleman. Maybe he's taking his time to make sure you're comfortable. I mean, the guy is from New York, you know? He's a little more sophisticated."

"More sophisticated than who?" asked Sonja defiantly.

"Than Denver boys," I answered, jumping off my bar stool and walking over to the fridge. "Than Vince. Than Maccabee. Derek's not trying to score as fast as he can. He's a slow burner. I think it's a good sign. I'm sure he'll come around and put the moves on our Cate. He'd be crazy not to."

"Hmm," sniffed Sonja, unconvinced. She took the bar stool next to Cate, poking at the journal with her fingernails. "I have a feeling that our little Cupid is losing his touch."

Cate shook her head. "It had to happen sometime."

"He'll come around," I said. "I know it."

"Oh, I'm hardly worried," said Cate. "I'm over it. Can we stop talking about it now? Why can't we talk about *you*, Sonja?"

"Yeah!" said Sonja. "Let's talk about *me*. Lucas, where's *my* Derek?"

"You don't need my help," I said. "You've got guys all over you."

"Like who?" protested Sonja.

"*Si una vez,*" I replied, smiling.

"Very funny, Lucas."

"What's that mean?" asked Cate.

Just then my cell started to vibrate. I snatched it from the special cell phone pocket on my jeans, got excited for a second that I was actually using my cell phone pocket, and flipped open the phone. "Hello?" I stood up, bashing my head on the cabinets that hung over the countertop. "Ouch."

"Lucas," said the voice. "Hey, baby. It's Derek."

"Hel-lo, Derek," I said, enunciating loudly to get the girls' attention. *Baby?* "How's it going?" Sonja stood up and walked over next to me.

"I'm good, man, thanks." His voice was so cute, deep but playful. "Good practice today. Hey, do you have Cate's number? I owe her a call and I can't find it."

A surge of disappointment hit my gut, and I fought to keep my face from falling. It took two long breaths to snuff the feeling before I could say, "Of course I do. But I have something better."

He laughed on the other end. "What's that, Lucas?"

"I've got Cate! Right here!"

I tossed the phone, hot-potato style, to Cate, who juggled it, struggling to hold on. "Lucas! I hate you!" she mouthed, then, "What do I say?"

I mimed putting the phone up to my ear and mouthed, "Hello?"

"Very funny," she said, raising the phone to her ear. "Hello? Hi, Derek . . . I'm good . . . Are you excited for Pueblo? . . . What? . . . This Saturday? . . . Um, okay . . . That sounds fun. . . . Okay, Saturday . . . Great! . . . What? . . . Okay, I'll tell him. . . . Okay, bye."

Cate flipped the phone closed, put it on the counter, and picked up her journal, testing the spine. Sonja and I just stared for a moment. *Okay, he's asked her out. He likes her. Okay. It's cool.* My heart was pounding so fast, I felt dizzy and had to rest my hand on the countertop. She'd said, 'I'll tell him.' . . . *Tell who? Me? Tell me what?*

"Okay, long enough," said Sonja, breaking the silence. "Spit."

Cate was blushing again. "He wants to go to another movie this weekend." She spun on her bar stool. "On Saturday."

Tell me what? That he wants me to come to the movie too? Tell me what?

"Right on, Derek!" cheered Sonja.

"You're right, Cate, I can tell you're totally over Derek." I forced myself to smirk. "Completely."

"Of course, I'm sure nothing will happen," said Cate. *Tell me what?* She threw the phone at me, still blushing. "Oh, and Lucas, he said to, quote, 'tell Mr. Handsome that I'll see him at practice tomorrow,' unquote. He just loves you, Lucas."

"What are you talking about?" I asked, shaking my head. "He's after you, not me."

I bit the inside of my cheek as soon as I said it. "Not *after*," I corrected myself. "You know what I mean."

"I didn't say he was *after* you, Lucas. I just said he *loves* you." She rolled her eyes at Sonja.

"Take me to your closet," said Sonja, grabbing Cate's arm and heading toward the stairs. "We need to start planning for Saturday. Lucas, *Mr. Handsome*, go watch TV." She pointed me toward the hallway that led past several bedrooms to the media room at the far end of Cate's sprawling ranch house.

"Just keep it down," said Cate. "I don't want to wake up Mom."

"Okay. And Sonja, remember, Cate's going out with Derek. Don't make her look too, you know, too *Denver*. Okay?"

"Relax, *mijo*," said Sonja. They walked out of the room.

I started down the hallway, looking forward to taking advantage of Cate's subscription to the Soccer Channel.

I flopped down on one of the long leather couches and flipped the remote to the Soccer Channel. They were showing a British match: Liverpool versus Manchester United. *He just loves you, Mr. Handsome.* Half an hour later, I was out cold, asleep on the couch.

Sometime later, I felt myself being covered up by a blanket. I moaned, half asleep, "Thanks, Mom."

"Ha!" came the response.

I flipped open my eyes and bolted up. "Where am I?" I yelped.

"Hey," whispered Julian.

The Soccer Channel was still on, now showing some match from Pakistan.

"Hi," I said, rubbing my eyes. "I must have fallen asleep." I shrank back onto the couch.

"Yeah, I guess," said Julian, sitting down on the other couch across from me and grabbing the remote. "You were snoring a little. But don't worry, it wasn't that bad. I didn't mind." He turned down the volume.

"Have you been here a long time?"

"Just for a little while, watching the match," he said. "Good match, too. The Pakistani goalie is great." He turned up the volume and watched another save. "Lucas, it's no sweat if you want to crash here. That's why I brought you that blanket."

"Thanks, man," I said. I arranged the blanket around my legs and tucked my feet under one of the cushions on the couch. "Julian, you would make such a good boyfriend. Why don't you have a girlfriend?"

"I don't know," he said, staring at the TV. "Just the way it is, I guess."

"You should have one," I said, sitting up again. "You could, you know. You're a soccer star. What about Tara MacIntyre?" I started filing through the girls in my head. "Or Jenny Jacobs. What's your type, anyway?"

Julian didn't answer, except to say, "Offsides!" to the TV.

"Lila Dunn?"

"Lucas," said Julian, not pulling his gaze from the TV. "How come you're always setting other people up? Why don't you find someone for yourself?"

I wasn't sure what to say. I didn't even have a joke. Not a quip. Nothing. I had no answer. So I didn't say anything.

"Nice save," said Julian to the TV.

11.

Sunday

"NO ME QUEDA MAS . . ." SANG SONJA AND SELENA AS SONJA crashed through the swinging door into the La Boca kitchen. "CCQ!" she yelled at Gabriel. "Twice! And a taquito appetizer, sauce on the side. *En mí corazón . . .* "

"Watch your back!" I barked at her, hoisting my tray of five entrées over my shoulder. "Coming through!" I slammed through the door and into the dining room, barely missing Cate, who was juggling a pot of coffee in one hand and a jug of water in the other. "Sorry!" I said. I stepped around a customer who'd just backed up his chair. "My bad." Cate didn't look up, staying on course for the wait station.

I skipped over a kid who was crawling around on the floor and nearly tripped over his mother, also crawling around. I managed to make it to table three without dropping a thing. Tonight was busy as *hell*. Since coming onto our shift at five, the three of us had been racing from table to table at breakneck speed. So far I'd turned over nine tables in three hours. A pain in the ass, but good for the tip pool.

I crashed back into the kitchen to continue the conversation we'd been having in spurts all evening. "I stayed in last night," I said, checking the hot deck for my orders. "To watch that *Swan* reunion special." I grabbed a corn chip from Cate's tray as she grazed past, staring at the ground. "You okay, Cate?" I asked. Her ponytail was sloppy tonight, her hair unwashed.

"Fine," she said. "Thanks."

"*¡Oye, Sonja!*" El Jefe called from the back stove, where he was stirring together a new batch of CCQ. "*¡Damelo . . . queso . . . alla!*" He pointed at a slab of cheese on the counter. She walked over and handed it to him. While most restaurants that serve CCQ melt their cheese in the microwave, El Jefe insisted on doing it stove top, even browning the bottom just slightly and stirring the brown bits throughout the cheese, lending a soft, smoky flavor to the mix. It required constant attention, and on busy nights like this, El Jefe never moved from his position at the stove. If he burned even one batch of CCQ, which *everyone* ordered, the whole evening would be thrown off. "*Te amo.*" He smiled at Sonja. "*Princesa.*"

She kissed him sweetly on the cheek, then turned back to me.

"Saturday night with *The Swan*, Lucas?" said Sonja, tearing a page off her order pad and tacking it onto the order board above Gabriel's station. "I had no idea you were such a baller. Were you sipping Cristal and getting lap dances too?"

"Oh, excuse me, Sandy Social Life," I said. "What did you get into last night?"

"Who cares?" she said. "I'm working on tonight. Have you seen the tank-top guy at table seven? Hottie."

"Sonja, that guy is here with his parents."

"My father always wanted me to marry a family man," said Sonja, readjusting her bra and lifting her boobs.

"*¡Oye, Sonja!*" yelped El Jefe from behind a pot of Mexican chicken soup. He stared at Sonja and wagged his finger. "Shhh!" He pointed at the photo of Sonja's mother above the stove.

Sonja sighed and wiped the hair from her forehead. She grabbed two handfuls of tortilla chips from the giant plastic bin underneath the stainless steel counter and tossed them into two red plastic baskets lined with waxed paper.

"Do two for me?" asked Cate, pointing at the chips. She was all business tonight. "I got salsa." She lined up four small white dishes, filling each one with a ladleful of salsa.

"Sonja, take it easy on table seven. You've got a shift to complete. And remember, Pueblo is next weekend. I'm sure there'll be plenty of fresh meat down there for you." Sonja groaned. I ignored her, turning my attention to Cate. "Your turn," I said, sliding my two pork verde entrées from the hot deck onto my tray. "What happened last night?"

"Yeah," said Sonja. "What happened with Derek?" She handed two baskets of chips to Cate, taking two bowls of salsa back. They each loaded their trays, hoisted them up, and turned to the door, which we all bashed through together.

"Nothing much," said Cate as we broke. We each went to a different area of the restaurant to deliver food.

Two minutes later, after refilling two tables' worth of ice water and picking up one chicken mole that had a hair in it, I was back in the kitchen with the girls.

"What do you mean, *nothing much*?" I said. "How was the movie?"

"It was fine," she said. "It was about this car that comes to life. I thought the ending was a little bit . . ."

"Cate," said Sonja, "we don't care how the movie was."

"No, seriously," said Cate, scooping guacamole onto a shell, building up a tostada del dia. "This guy had to save the world from this evil car. . . ."

"Cate!" I shouted. "Derek?"

Cate shrugged. "I don't know. Nothing, really."

"Come on," I demanded. "Not even a kiss?"

Cate shook her head before she spoke, saying only, "Nope. Nothing." She looked at her feet. "You guys, I even tried this time! I practically jumped him when he dropped me off. Leaned over from the passenger seat, grabbed his head, and kissed him, straight on the lips. And he let me! But he didn't kiss me back. He didn't even turn his head toward me. It was like kissing a CPR dummy. He just said, 'Good night, Cate. I really had a good time.' I've never felt so rejected," she sniffled. "I actually thought we had something in common. He likes Wegman!"

Cate looked at me. "Lucas? What gives?" she asked, as if *I* could explain it. "Why doesn't he want to kiss me?"

I held up my hands. "Got me," I said. Deep in my stomach there was a fluttering. Was it disappointment? Excitement? Guilt? Hope? I couldn't tell.

"It sucks," said Cate.

"Well, you shouldn't be too bummed, right?" I said with forced brightness. I reached my arm around her and gave her a squeeze. "You never really liked him that much anyway. So, no big loss."

Sonja reached over to slap the side of my head. "Idiot! Can't you see that she likes him!"

"Yeah, dick," said Cate. "That's what sucks. The more your stupid little idea fails and nothing happens with Derek, the more I'm starting to like him. I don't know what it is."

I know what it is, I thought. *He's amazing. Anyone would fall in love with him.*

"He's just," said Cate, "something else."

Sonja leaned forward, hanging on Cate's words.

"Yeah," I said. "I know." I was biting my tongue to keep from agreeing too emphatically. "But whatever. He's not all that."

"Yes, he is, Lucas," said Cate, lowering her voice. "He's different. You can see it when he's on the field. He plays soccer like a man, not some high school kid."

"That's almost exactly what you said about Vince," I said. "You went out with him because of his soccer skills."

"Thanks for reminding me," said Cate. "Please never mention that name again."

"At least Vince put out," said Sonja. "Just kidding."

"Nice, Sonja," said Cate, glaring. She was blushing crimson now. I saw a tear beginning to form in the corner of her eye. "That's not funny."

"Oh, sweetie," said Sonja. "I'm just kidding." She put her arm around Cate. "Wow, you're really bumming."

"It sucks. He grabs at the guys on the team more than he grabs at me. *Julian* gets more action from him during practice than I do on a date," said Cate, wiping her eye and catching her breath. "What am I doing wrong?"

"Order up!" barked Gabriel from the stove. We sprang to the hot deck to grab our orders.

"You're not doing anything wrong," I said, grabbing a too-hot combination plate. "Ouch!" I shook my finger. "Maybe he's just, I don't know, *too* perfect. You know?" I spun around, tray up, and headed through the door and into the dining room.

After delivering the combination plate to one table and picking up the check and a credit card from another, I was back in the kitchen, sucking on my burned finger.

"Too perfect for what?" hissed Cate, who hadn't moved from the order-up counter. "Are you saying I'm not good enough for him? What is that supposed to mean, Lucas?"

"No!" I shushed, handing the check and credit card to Sonja, who took them out front to ring up. "That's not what I mean. Take it easy! I'm just saying he's from New York, you know?"

"Taquitos!" shouted Gabriel.

"So you mean," said Cate, her voice tense, "that I'm too *Denver* for him?"

"I didn't say that," I said. Sonja was back, holding Cate's hand, and glaring at me. "I didn't mean that."

Cate wiggled free from Sonja and started to pace in front of the hot deck, which was now nearly full of plates ready to go out. "Lucas, for someone who's supposed to be my best friend, you can be a real asshole sometimes." She started loading up her tray, slamming plates down. "This whole thing was your idea in the first place. So, what now, Lucas? Are you saying I should just forget about Derek?" She clenched her fists. "*No big loss*, was it?" She looked up at me. "I hate feeling this way! And it's your fault."

"Look," I said, panicking slightly, "just give me some time to get closer to him. I'll figure him out."

"What do you mean, *figure him out?*" asked Cate. "Figure what out?" She tipped her head to the side.

"He just means," said Sonja, "that we don't know that much about Derek when it really comes down to it. I mean, maybe there's some reason he acts the way he does. The guy could be gay for all we know, right?"

"Sonja!" I snapped.

"No way." Cate shook her head vigorously. "He's not gay. He can't be. He used to have a girlfriend in New York."

"Order up!" shouted Gabriel from behind the now-overflowing hot deck. "Sonja, these enchiladas are yours!

I need space up here!" Sonja and I backed toward the hot deck.

"Wait a minute," said Cate accusingly. She didn't move. "You *do* think he's gay, don't you, Lucas?"

"No," I said. "I don't. I don't know what I think." I really didn't. For all I knew, Derek was into farm animals. I just knew that I didn't know how I felt. And that my head was spinning. But for a reason I couldn't quite place, I was pissed. "I still don't get why you care so much. Unless you *slept* with him."

"*¡Ay!*" shouted Gabriel. El Jefe just kept stirring. I wondered if he could hear us.

"Yeah, right, like that would ever happen," said Cate.

"Don't you mean 'like that would ever happen . . . again'?" I said. "Are we forgetting what happened with Vince?"

"Cate?" gasped Sonja. "You slept with Vince? I didn't know that!"

I lost my breath and my stomach dropped when I realized I'd just revealed too much. Of course Sonja didn't know. Cate had made me promise not to tell anyone. But I just had. My anger and frustration were washed away in a wave of instant, panicked regret. "Cate, I didn't mean . . ."

Cate just stood, suddenly calm. She squared her shoulders and intensified her stare. "You didn't mean what?" she demanded, eyes intense, twitching. "Lucas, what are you up to? What is this really about?" She swiped at her face, flicking the last tear from her cheek.

"What do you mean?" I asked. "I'm not up to anything."

"Oh, please, Lucas. You're always up to something. What's your little scheme this time? Are you using me to get to him?"

"It's not like that!" I snapped back. "Why would I do that?"

"You think he's gay," snarled Cate. "You want him for yourself. You gay guys are all the same. You think *everyone's* gay."

"Screw *that*, Cate," I said. "I am *not* that person. I don't like him like that!" I started loading up my tray with plates, one after the other. "I can't believe what a bigot you are." I kept stacking plates. My tray was getting heavier by the instant, and still I kept stacking.

"Oh my God," said Sonja. "You two are freaking me out." She pushed her way through the swinging door out of the room.

Cate still hadn't moved. "A bigot? At least I'm not a snake, Lucas. Why are you managing the soccer team, anyway?" She was speaking slowly, still not moving. "Sonja needs the PE credit. But you don't. So why?"

"To be with Sonja," I said, stacking another plate. Was it even mine? I didn't care. "Because she asked me to. Because friends do that."

"Is that right? To be with Sonja?" she asked, shaking her head. "Or was it to be with him?"

One more plate.

"You are in love with Derek, and you used me to get to him. That's what you did."

"I DID NOT!" I yelled, grabbing the last plate from the order-up station and slamming it onto my tray. Instantly I felt it start to shift, and I felt my plates slide to one side. I bent down at the knee, trying to shift my balance underneath the tray and save the plates, but it was too late. They'd gained too much momentum. My tray slid from my hands, sending the stack of plates crashing to the floor, shattering.

The kitchen, except for the Mexican soccer announcer on the tiny little black-and-white TV over by the sink, went quiet. El Jefe stopped stirring. Gabriel stopped plating. Even the din from the dining room stopped for a moment. It was that loud.

The floor was covered now in a sharp, slippery layer of food and porcelain.

"You *used* your best friend. That's what you did." Cate put her tray down, untied her apron, and took the pencil out of her ponytail. "I thought you were on my side," she said, walking out the door. "Don't ever speak to me again, Lucas. I mean that. Ever. You are a terrible person."

"Cate, stop . . . You don't mean . . ." I held out my hands.

"Oh yes, yes, I do," sputtered Cate, quiet and terse. "You are *not* my friend. I'm out of here."

She shuffled into the parking lot, limping more heavily than I'd seen in a while. Moments later, she was driving away.

"Order up!" shouted Gabriel, who began cursing in Spanish. *Shut up,* I thought.

Sonja burst through the swinging door. "Where's Cate

going?" she demanded. "Cate!" She ran to the back door and looked out into the parking lot. Cate's red taillights flickered in the distance.

"She's gone," I said. "She's crazy. What's wrong with her?"

"I don't know what the hell is wrong with either one of you," said Sonja, pushing past me toward the hot deck and gesturing feverishly. "Ever since Freddy Fantastic showed up, it's nonstop drama around here. And what you don't get is, he is *so* not worth the drama! He's just another guy!" She threw her hair to one side. "*¡Nada!*"

"He *is* different, Sonja," I said, at her heels. "And besides, what if he and Cate really *do* get together? Isn't that worth it?" I threw my hands up, like a beggar.

"Lucas," said Sonja, "give it up." She started methodically loading her tray. "Gabriel! Get the mop. Papa!" she yelled. "We need help over here!"

12.

Friday

IT HAD BEEN FIVE DAYS SINCE OUR FIGHT.

All week long, I'd been obsessing about the fight, worrying about what I'd said, what Cate had meant, how I'd hurt her, how she'd hurt me. I couldn't tell what the truth was. All I could really remember, clearly, was my best friend telling me she never wanted to see me again.

I'd betrayed her, and she wanted me out of her life.

Maybe I *was* the terrible friend she said I was. Maybe I had been using her to get to Derek. But I hadn't meant to. I'd been trying to get them together! Sort of.

I didn't know anymore. It had been five days, and she and I still weren't speaking.

I'd been doing my best to avoid Derek too, pretending not to see him at school and staying just out of reach at practice. I wanted to clear my head of him.

"Crazy, both of you. Fighting over a guy. Please, how retarded," Sonja was saying. "Here, take this. Wake up!"

I shook my head and remembered where I was: outside the locker room, loading up Mom's Subaru for the drive to Pueblo. As team managers, we were responsible for six extra soccer balls, eighteen extra sets of shin pads, two first-aid kits, a defibrillator, and two large orange coolers for mixing Gatorade.

"And these," said Sonja. She was holding out a black nylon bag. "Can you count them? We need thirty-six."

"What are they?" I asked.

"Protective cups," said Sonja. "And I'm not going near them, so don't even try it." She unzipped her An/Gel hoodie, exposing a baby blue tank top, and fanned her face with her free hand.

"How are we doing on logistics? Do you have the roster lists?" I asked, peering into the bag. "And the vouchers for the hotel?" Sonja had been responsible for our reservations at the Holiday Inn. I would room with Julian, and Sonja, as the only girl on the whole trip, would get her own room. We already had plans for me to sneak into her room and watch movies. "What about the schedule of play?"

"One thing at a time, *mijo*!" She held open her shoulder bag with one hand, digging through with the other. "*Ay*, logistics . . ." She waved a clipboard stacked full of loose papers. "Rosters! And schedules!"

"Vouchers?" I wondered if I'd see much of Derek this weekend. Would we hang out? See each other? Eat together? Party together?

"Vouchers . . ." Sonja muttered, dunking her head in her purse. "Vouchers . . ."

Behind her, Coach Le Beouf was directing the team onto the bus. Julian waved at me from the back of the line of players. "Hey, Sonja!" yelled one of the players. "I'll be in room three thirty-two!"

"Go to hell," she muttered without even looking up. And that was it. "Vouchers . . ."

I could see Derek up front, punching at the keys of his cell phone. I wondered who he was calling and wished it was me.

"No cell phones on the bus, Griffin," said Coach. "School policy."

I was looking forward to the drive down with Sonja. We'd hit a drive-through or two and listen to the radio the whole way down. There'd be no drama. No Cate. Just us.

"¡Ay!" she yelled, right arm elbow deep in her purse. She pulled it out, clutching a manila envelope. "Vouchers!"

"Nice job, Patsy Paperwork," I said. "Now, could you bring me up a tuna sandwich?"

"Very funny," said Sonja, zipping her hoodie.

"Hey!" shouted Coach Le Beouf, hanging out of the bus door. "Lewis!"

I figured he meant me. "Yeah?"

"Arrive alive!" He backed into the bus as the driver pulled the lever that closed the door.

"Okay, Coach!"

We climbed into the Subaru and followed the bus out of the parking lot and onto Hampden Avenue. I saw Vince in the back window of the bus, checking his skin in the reflection in the window. He reached up and plucked a hair from one of his eyebrows.

"Ugh," I said. "Are we going to have to watch that the whole way down?"

"We can lose 'em," said Sonja as my phone started to ring. I dug it out of my jeans and handed it to Sonja. "Who is it?"

She checked the caller ID, then flipped open the phone. "Julian? It's Sonja. What's up on the bus? . . . What? . . . Where are you? . . . You went to pee? . . . They left? . . . Who are you with? . . . *Ay*, Julian, are you crazy? Didn't Coach notice? . . . Okay, we're coming to get you. Stay there!" She flipped the phone closed.

"Julian went to pee and—" started Sonja.

I held up one hand. "I got it," I said, already making a right to circle back to the TJ parking lot. "We can pick up Julian, no problem. I mean, the team needs him, right?" I smiled. "He'll probably just fall asleep anyway."

I pulled into the parking lot where we'd just loaded up. "Where is he?" I asked Sonja, looking around.

"Here he comes," said Sonja, pointing at the entrance to the gym. "Here they come."

They? There was Julian, in his worn-out Birks, walking toward the car, oversized gym bag hoisted over his shoulder. Next to him was Cate. I sat straight up in the Subaru, bashing my head on the roof.

"Oh no," I said. "Oh no, you didn't."

"But we can't play without a goalie, Lucas," said Sonja, unbuckling her seat belt. "He has to be there."

"Him, yes." I nodded emphatically. "Her, no. Sonja, I can't deal. No."

"Lucas! You're being stupid! She's your best friend!" She snapped in the air. "Get over it!"

"Forget it," I said. "She can take a Greyhound or something."

Sonja sighed. I could feel her studying my profile. She grabbed my forearm with one hand and my chin with the other. "She needs to be in Pueblo," said Sonja. "For Julian."

I gripped the steering wheel tighter. "Not my problem," I said. "The answer is *no!*"

"Fine, you can say no," said Sonja. "It's your car. But," she said, her eyes burning, her nails digging into my forearm, "please? For me?"

"What do you care? What difference does it make to you?"

"It's just a two-hour drive."

I smacked the steering wheel with both hands. "You set this up," I said. She didn't answer. "Fine." What else could I do? She'd trapped me.

I turned off the engine and climbed out to open the Subaru's hatchback. "I'm not sure how much room we have," I told Julian, shaking my head. I ignored Cate.

I climbed back into the driver's seat and pushed on my sunglasses.

Julian walked around to my side of the car and leaned his head in my window. "You gonna make it?" he asked.

"Ask again later," I said, reaching for the radio. I kept it on full blast the whole trip down so none of us could talk to one another.

It wasn't until I-25 just past Colorado Springs that I

started wondering what would happen when we won the tournament, and Derek got drunk at the victory party and hooked up with Cate at the Holiday Inn. What would happen when they kissed?

The thought made my stomach jump and my pulse race. I wanted to erase it. But I wanted even more to torture myself with the thought, to follow it through, all the way to the cuddling after they finished.

And this sharp voice in the back of my head kept repeating, *Isn't that what you wanted in the first place?*

13.

Friday

"WE MADE IT," SAID JULIAN. WE STEPPED OFF THE ELEVATOR and made a left. Our "suite," 504, was just off the fifth-floor elevator bank, directly across from a small, brightly lit room crowded with vending machines and a huge, jet-engine-roar ice maker. Three high school guys in nylon sweatpants, soccer T-shirts, and flip-flops shuffled past us.

"Are all the teams staying at the Holiday Inn?" I asked Julian.

"Nah," he said, offering no further explanation. He slipped his key card into the slot. The green light flashed on, and Julian popped the door open.

"Hey!" came a familiar voice. "Is that you?"

I knew it was Derek. But when Julian looked at me quizzically, I shrugged. I held the door while he wrangled his bag through, past the bathroom, down the short hallway, and around the corner into the room. I followed, letting the door slam behind me. I peeked into the bathroom, shelves stacked high with white-and-green towels.

I rounded the corner and there was Derek—shirtless, in sweats, lying on one of the two beds, remote in one hand, Coca-Cola in the other. *What's he doing here?*

"Hey," he said. "What happened to you, Julian?"

"Got left," said Julian. "What's up?"

"Chilling," said Derek. "Waiting on you guys." He pointed at the TV, where Carmen Electra was cavorting in a bikini. "She's hot," he said. "That body." He put the remote on his stomach, then raised one arm behind his head. He looked up at me and grinned. "Hey, man."

"Hey, man," I said. I tried to concentrate on the TV to keep from staring. I turned to Julian. "Are we in the right room?" I asked.

"Yeah!" said Derek, jumping up. "You're in the right place! I guess we were two rooms short or something, so I volunteered to be transferred into your room. Sweet, huh!" He high-fived Julian, then me. "I hope one of you doesn't mind sharing a bed." He reached down to readjust himself through his sweats.

"I'll take the couch!" I said quickly. "I need to pee!"

I dropped my bag on the couch and ducked into the bathroom, locking the door. I turned on the water and spun free a length of toilet paper. The fluorescent light cast a cloudy white glow over the whole room. I blew my nose, tossed the tissue, and stared myself down in the mirror. My eyes were bloodshot, my skin flushed. I had lines in my forehead, like I'd been furrowing my brow so hard the lines stuck.

I'm rooming with Derek.

I sucked in my breath, filling my lungs deeply, and said it aloud. "I'm rooming with Derek."

I wasn't ready for this. *I'm probably going to see him naked!* I thought. *What do I do? How do I act? What do I say? What if they can hear me pee? What if I fart in the middle of the night?*

I listened to myself, getting angry. This wasn't the kind of thing that *guys* freak out about when they room with other guys. Because if you're straight, that woody doesn't really mean anything. If you're gay, suddenly everyone's afraid.

As out as I was, there were still places in the world, and times, when I wished I wasn't out at all. There were times I wished I wasn't gay.

Relax, I thought. *Take it easy. You know these guys. They like you. Don't freak. Just relax. Be one of the guys. At least you're not rooming with Vince.*

I splashed some water on my face. Too hot. I reached to adjust the temperature. *I can deal with Julian. He's practically family. But Derek?* I splashed again, then pressed a towel against my face.

I felt conspicuous. Alone. And really, really *gay*.

Being myself this weekend was out of the question.

You have no choice, I thought. *There's no way out.* Cate was staying with Sonja, so there was no refuge there. I'd have to stay quiet, lie low, and stick to the background. I'd have to breathe deep and keep my eyes on the TV. I'd have to be patient and not count the hours. I could handle it.

I washed my hands, shut off the water, and walked back

out into the room. Derek and Julian were each on a bed, holding up cans of Coke in a toast.

"Want a Coke?" asked Derek, jumping up to open the mini-fridge under the desk. "We topped ours off with a little Jack." He held up a smallish bottle of whiskey. "Tastes better that way."

"Sure," I said. "Why not?"

"Attaboy," said Derek, pouring. He handed me my can of Coke.

I cleared my throat. "As team manager, I am required to remind you that you are not to be hungover tomorrow, boys," I said, raising my can. "To victory tomorrow."

"To victory!" said Derek, raising his can.

I drank, and I liked it. Sure, maybe I wished there'd been a garnish, maybe a cherry or an orange slice, but hey. *Just one of the guys here.* I laughed at myself. *Can't wait for SportsCenter.*

I took another sip and settled onto the couch. For the next ten minutes, none of us talked at all, and it was great. Derek just flipped from station to station, taking us on a journey through news, videos, ESPN, even the Food Network. Julian and I just sipped our drinks, quiet.

I wondered what the girls were doing.

Just then there was a banging at the door. A guy's voice came through. "Griffin! Get out here! Hey! Griffin!" Another voice joined his. "Yeah, Griffin! We know you're in there! Open up!"

Derek stood up. "They're crazy." He shook his head.

"Griffin! Dude! You have to do shots with us!" yelled yet

a third voice. "It's tradition! It's your first Pueblo!" Several voices chimed in, all bristling and urgent. They were chanting, "Drink! Drink! Drink! Drink!"

"Let me go see what these jokers want," said Derek, pulling on a T-shirt with a photo-print of a samurai warrior on the front. I watched from the couch as he peeked through the peephole in the door. "Oh, man," he said, laughing. He opened up.

A burst of players streamed into the room. *So much for SportsCenter.* I jumped up off the couch and moved back toward the window, next to the mismatched drapes. Not to hide, just to fade. Someone turned the TV up to full blast. It was a familiar infomercial concerning hair regrowth.

"Griffin! You must drink! Don't be gay!" they were shouting. "Partyyyy!!" They were falling all over each other like crazed fans in a mass grab, like girls at a Justin Timberlake concert.

Instantly our room became a full-on party. The entire TJ team was in there, high-fiving, whooping, jumping on the beds, drinking from bottles wrapped in brown paper.

"Oh, I boned Christina," said one voice. "She was all over it, man, losing control and moaning."

"Why aren't there any girls on this trip?" said another. "I need a hummer!"

"Isn't that Sonja's job?" A third voice snickered. "As team manager and all?" Vince. *Dick.* I wished Sonja were here to cut him down.

I pulled the curtain back just far enough to see what was going on.

Vince carried a plastic cup and a bottle over to Derek. "Attention, please!" yelled Vince. "This is the first time in Pueblo for our newest *superstar*, Derek Griffin." He poured out a shot of what looked like tequila and handed it to Derek. "Therefore, as tradition demands, he must drink." He started chanting slowly, "Drink! . . . Drink! . . . Drink!"

A couple of other players joined in. "Drink! . . . Drink! . . ." Soon the entire room was in a frenzied chant. "Drink! Drink! Drink! Drink!"

"Tradition," said Derek, staring at Vince before tossing his head back and pouring the shot down his throat. He handed his cup back to Vince. "Is that all you've got?"

The room cheered.

I faded myself into a space in the corner, behind Julian's bed, half obscured by the mismatched orange curtain. Ducking behind the musty curtain, I looked out the window into the parking lot, flanked by an Applebee's sign and a Taco John's. *Great,* I thought. *Nice view.*

"TJ sucks! TJ sucks!" came a competing round of chanting, loud, from out in the hallway. "Canon City rules!" An empty beer can came flying in from the entrance, crashing to the floor.

The room went quiet for a moment, and the guys outside the room bolted. Derek raced to the door in mock pursuit, Vince and the others trailing behind him like tentacles.

Derek stopped short of the hallway. Vince pushed past him, shouting, "Pussies!" after the Canon City boys. The rest of the boys followed him. I figured this was part of the ritual.

And as quickly as it had descended, the party bolted out into the hallway. Julian, lagging behind, joined the swell. And then the room was empty. The beds were rumpled; pillows were torn out of their cases. Towels and plastic cups littered the floor. The TV was blaring the same infomercial for hair renewal. And I was still hiding—no, just fading—behind the curtain.

I supposed I could have gone with them, but I stayed back. I'd shut the door and watch some TV. It just seemed better that way. I poured some more Jack Daniels into my Coke and sat down on Derek's bed. I grabbed the remote.

I must have been really tired, because I don't even remember falling asleep.

14.

Friday

WHAT WOKE ME UP FIRST WAS THE WARM BREATH ON MY NECK. Even, deep, and heavy.

I started to come to consciousness but only made it halfway. Where was I? I knew I wasn't at home. But where? Deep in the fog of half sleep, I was lost.

Then I smelled the Jack Daniels.

I forced my eyes open, which made no difference. I still couldn't see, and I still couldn't move. The room was totally dark. I could just barely make out my own hand, which was resting on the mattress in front of me.

I reached up to scratch my nose. Only my hand didn't move. Something wasn't right. I rubbed my eyes and looked again. It was still there, resting on the mattress. *Am I dreaming?*

When I put my hand back down, grazing the hand on the mattress, I realized two things—I wasn't dreaming. And also, the hand on the mattress wasn't mine.

There was an arm draped over my side. There was a leg pressing up against the back of mine. And there was a foot thrown over my ankle, only I couldn't see that far. It was too dark.

I felt the rise and fall of the Jack Daniels breath, coating my back in a mist.

I am being spooned.

Still coming to consciousness, it took another second or two to finish the thought. I looked back at the hand on the mattress, and as my eyes began to adjust, I recognized the outline of a black Swiss Army watch with a green glowing dial.

I am being spooned. By Derek.

Oh.

My.

God.

Okay, this was major. How did I get here? What was going on? I began a panicked assessment, afraid of what I might find. Whatever this meant, I wasn't prepared for it.

I noted that I was fully clothed. *Okay, good sign.*

I determined that we were on top of, not in, his bed. *Good.*

I turned my head slowly to see what he was wearing. It took me a minute of squinting through the dark to put it together. Boxers. No shirt. *Not so good.*

He looked beautiful, perfect, like a man, not a boy.

I put the pieces together slowly. It all seemed pretty harmless. I'd fallen asleep watching TV on his bed. He'd stumbled in, drunk. He'd crashed on the bed next to me. There was no way he'd known what he was doing.

The only thing was, he wasn't just snoring away next to me. He was spooning me. Holding on hard.

Take it easy. It's not like he's trying to make out with you, I told myself. *He's trashed. He's just having a dream about some girl, and he grabbed you in his sleep. He'd be doing the same to his dog.*

But he wasn't spooning his dog. He wasn't spooning some girl, not even Cate. He was spooning *me.* Lucas. And it felt amazing. Scary—panic-inducing, in fact—but it made me feel like I mattered.

His arm, strong and lean, was tucked around my chest, grasping my arm. His leg, the leg I'd watched intently every day at practice, mesmerized by its power, was now pressed up against mine. His foot, magical on the field, was tossed over mine. Derek was wrapped around me, was comfortable, sleeping, open. I didn't want to move.

Ever.

Afraid to wake him, afraid that would end the embrace, I concentrated on staying still in the dark. I felt an itch surface on my back, but I made no move to scratch it. I felt another surface on my knee, but I willed it back. I would not move. And then a horrible guilty thought popped into my head. *He's Cate's. He's supposed to be Cate's.* But if he was with me, obviously he wasn't Cate's. He was never hers at all.

And that's when, in a panic, I remembered something else: *Julian!*

I strained to hear another set of lungs. *Is he here?*

I took a deep, silent breath, then concentrated on matching my breathing to Derek's. I wanted to lie awake all night, breathing with him, not scratching my itches. Every few breaths, I curled my head back slightly, millimeter by millimeter, nudging the nape of my neck against where I imagined his face to be.

I counted the steady Jack Daniels breaths until the first shards of light wedged their way through the worn blackout shades. That's when I raised my head, looking across the gap between the beds. There, just four feet away, lay Julian.

Are his eyes open? I wondered. *What do I do? Do I say hi? Do I pretend to be asleep? Do I get up and go to the couch?* I dropped my head back to the bed. *Now what?*

I decided to move to the couch. More than anything in the world I didn't want to, but somehow I knew I had to. Carefully I picked up Derek's hand. I moved it gingerly up and off. I placed it behind me. I gently slid my foot out from under his. Slowly I shifted my weight, sitting up. I looked over at Julian, who'd turned over and was now facing the other way.

Had he seen us?

I dropped my foot to the floor as lightly as I could. I inhaled, preparing to pull myself up slowly, steadily, off the bed. I didn't want to jar Derek awake.

Suddenly I felt his arm, heavy, strong, and peach fuzzed, swing back around me. "No," he grunted. "No, don't go."

Derek pulled me back down, spooning me again. He curled his chest against my back and raised his knee up behind mine. He pressed forward against my hip, gripping my body insistently, like a baby who doesn't want to be put down.

I felt his lips against my neck. And this time, I wasn't imagining it. Derek pulled me even closer as his breaths evened out. I felt my body disintegrate in his arms.

Maybe he's not that drunk. Maybe he knows exactly what he's doing.

"Stay here," he mumbled, eyes closed. "Stay."

15.

Saturday

THE WHOLE BED SHOOK, WAKING ME VIOLENTLY. I BOLTED upright as I heard the bathroom door slam shut.

I could see Julian in the corner of the room, quietly pulling up his sweats and putting on his socks.

So he'd seen us.

I figured Derek was in the bathroom. He'd probably just jumped out of bed in horror and barricaded himself in there. He'd crossed a line he didn't want to cross and was now freaking out. I could feel his anger, his disgust. He needed to know that it was nothing. He needed to know it wasn't his fault.

I wanted desperately to tell him. But I wasn't that brave. I closed my eyes again, pretending to sleep.

16.

Saturday

I SPOTTED SONJA DEEP IN THE SIDELINE CROWD, WHICH WAS heavy with soccer parents carrying silver portable coffee cups and flaunting their latest Polartec separates. She was struggling to drag an orange cooler of Gatorade through the crowd to the players' area on the sidelines. Her hair was spilling out from under a blue bandanna, draped over her face and neck and falling in her eyes. Her sweats were wet halfway up the back of her legs like they'd been dragging behind her all morning. Her hoodie drooped.

I took a deep breath and thrust out my hand.

"Let me help," I said, grabbing one handle of the cooler. Sonja huffed, sighed, and took up the other handle while shaking her head. A cheer came from one of the three fields behind us. The Pueblo All-State complex, just east of the imposing Sangre de Cristo mountain range, had a total of eight full-size soccer fields. All eight would be heavily used today. "Let's go," I said, nodding toward the bench.

"You better have a damn good excuse for not having been here this morning," she said, kicking up stray sideline chalk with her flip-flop. I watched a cloud of it catch a breeze, rise above our heads and disappear against the gray sky. "I had to set up everything by myself."

"Sonja, I'm sorry."

"Just so you know, you're cleaning up by yourself tonight. As soon as that last game is over, I'm out of here. Win or lose."

"Deal," I said. "I suck. If I had a tail, I'd tuck it between my legs." I couldn't believe I'd actually fallen back asleep this morning. *What the hell happened last night?*

We reached the players' area and hoisted the Gatorade up onto the card table Sonja had set up next to the bench. "Lucas, no offense, but you look like hell," she said. "Are you okay?"

Just then, a cheer went up on the opposing sideline. "I guess they agree," I said.

"Seriously, Lucas. Maybe you should sit." She drew me a cup of Gatorade.

"I'm fine," I said, lying. I sat on the bench. "Mmm, grape."

Then I saw him. Derek. Beautiful, mysterious Derek. *Stay,* he'd said.

He was standing just in front of the penalty box, bouncing

from one cleated foot to the other, focused intently on the action. He sprang into a sprint for three steps, then stopped and ran back, swaggering like he owned the field, which he did. "Nice!" he yelled. "Move up! Now! Nice shot, DiSimone!"

He turned to Coach Le Beouf on the sidelines and threw his arm into the air in frustration. I remembered how strong that arm had felt this morning, pulling me closer to him in bed. "Shoot, Vince!"

Behind Derek, standing just in front of the goal, was Julian. And as intense and clear-minded as Derek seemed on the field, Julian seemed even more so. He stood, catlike, on his toes, knees bent, slinky, with his fingers outstretched. His eyes were set solidly, searingly on the ball. His lips moved in an inaudible mumble as he slowly shuffled back and forth.

Suddenly a cheer came up from the other end of the field, and both Derek and Julian sprang into motion, racing forward. "Gooooal!" I spun my head around. "Yeah!!"

The entire team rushed Vince, who'd just torn off his shirt and was waving it around in victory. The crowd on the sidelines, jubilant, did an impromptu wave.

"Wow," said Sonja, nodding.

"Are you wowing the goal?" I asked. "Or Vince's abs?"

"A little of each," said Sonja, snapping a towel at me. "He may be a dick, but he has his assets." She lowered her sunglasses. "Mmm."

"Sonja," I said, "you are such a ho."

"Eat it, Lucas," said Sonja. "Besides, if you'd hook me up with Mike Maccabee already, I'd be a one-man girl. By the way, in addition to clearing up this morning, that Mike thing is back on. *¿Entiendes?*"

"Yeah, right," I said. "A one-man girl."

Sonja threw her hand up in my face. "Watch it."

The halftime horn blew, and the players came jogging off the field to the bench. A flood of outstretched hands, powered by muddy legs, galloped toward us.

"Lucas!" I heard. It was Vince, still receiving back slaps and congratulations, yelling impatiently. "Gatorade!" He was all business today, ready to win. No snide comments, not even about Sonja.

Head down, I walked swiftly over to the cooler and drew a cup. "Grape," I said, not looking up as I held it out.

"Thanks," came a voice, not Vince's.

Derek.

I looked up, slowly dragging my eyes along his body, from cleats to shin pads to shorts to jersey to neck to jaw to lips to nose, but I never made it to his eyes. I was too afraid of what I'd see. . . . Rejection? Fear? Pity? Hate?

Love?

"Grape," he said.

"Yup," I said, wishing I could say, "I love you."

"I love grape," he said, voice animated. "Can I have some more?" He held out his cup. I remembered how his breath had felt on my neck.

"Derek! Derek!" came a voice from behind me. I knew it was Cate's instantly. "You rock!" Derek looked up and smiled.

"Hey, Cate!" he said, holding out his arms.

Pushing her way through the team, she came and stood in between me and Derek. "Nice job!" she said, standing on her tiptoes and kissing him just to the side of his mouth. He slapped his hand over his cheek.

"Thanks," he said, feigning shyness.

"Watch their left wing," she said, pointing at the other team. "He's good."

"I will," he said, still smiling. She rumpled his hair.

"Did you get any sleep?" she asked.

"I'm not sure," he answered. "You?" His eyes were searching hers, sparkling.

"Not a wink," she said, screwing her face up in mock anger. "Thanks to you." She pushed him away.

"Griffin!" barked Coach Le Beouf. Derek trotted off.

Cate turned and looked at me. "Hi, Lucas. I didn't see you there." She looked over my shoulder and spotted Julian. "Hey, bro!" she yelled, stepping around me.

I was dizzy. *Did you get any sleep?* What was that supposed to mean?

I hadn't seen Cate like this since Vince. *Not since Vince.*

I sat back, luckily landing on the bench just behind me. I wasn't sure what I'd just seen. Something wasn't right. Something had changed.

"Sonja," I croaked, looking around for her. "Sonja?" I sprang up, pacing now. I had to know.

I saw her bent over the cooler, mixing up a new batch of Gatorade. "Sonja," I said, lunging at her. "Do you know something I don't?"

Sonja kept stirring.

"Sonja," I said. "Come *on*. I just want to know. I'll be psyched!" I could hear the words coming out of my mouth sounding so forced, so utterly desperate. "This is what we wanted!"

"Look," she said, pushing hair out of her eyes. "You and Cate have your thing with Derek. Leave me out of it." She tore off her bandanna, releasing her hair in every direction. She tore at the knot in frustration. "This thing sucks!"

"Sonja," I hissed. "Tell me." I grabbed the bandanna and stuck the knot in my teeth, loosening it. "Here," I said, shaking it out. She grabbed it back.

She folded the bandanna into a triangle and tied it on.

"Did they hook up?" I demanded, stealing the bandanna away again.

"I don't know!" She pushed my hand away and stole back the bandanna.

I spun away. *They couldn't have hooked up,* I thought. *He was with me!* I panicked quietly on the bench. *He was with me.* I watched the action from behind my sunglasses. After every play he made, Derek turned to look at Cate, who was pacing behind our goal. Cate responded with a clap and a thumbs-up each time.

I hated myself for staying behind last night. What had happened?

"Gooooal!"

The game finished off. We won, 2–0. The next game was also decisive, a 4–0 win over Alamosa. Julian, with two shutouts under his belt, was dubbed "Hero Goalkeeper" by Coach Le Beouf.

And my panic mellowed into a slow burn as I drifted between hating myself for staying in Derek's bed this morning to hating myself for not going out last night to hating myself for hating myself. Woven through the self-hate was Cate hate, Sonja hate, and soccer hate. But never Derek hate.

By late afternoon, as the shadows from the Sangre de Cristo range stretched across the field, we were locked in a tense match for the championship with Canon City. With only minutes left to go, the game was scoreless, a draw that was frustrating both teams and spectators. Derek, Julian, and the other players were tired but continued to pace the field, determined to find an opening, determined to score. As the game went on, I'd noticed Derek looking at Cate less and less, no matter how she cheered or gestured. With each play, he was even more focused on the game.

"Move up!" yelled Derek, swinging his arms and sprinting forward. He pointed at Vince, who was bearing down on Canon City's goalie with the ball at his toes. "DiSimone's over the goal line!" The TJ backfield sprinted up with him. "Put some pressure on them!"

Vince shot the ball into the top corner of the goal, only to have it knocked out of bounds by their goalie. A moan went through the sideline crowd as the final horn sounded. The score was 0–0.

"Now what?" said Sonja flatly.

"You know," I said, also completely without emotion. "A shoot-out. Each team gets five free shots on goal, with no defenders besides the goalie. Whichever team scores the most goals out of those five shots wins."

"Really?" said Sonja. "That's what it comes down to?"

"That's why it sucks to be Julian. It sucks to be the goalie," I said.

"Good thing he's so good," said Sonja. "And check out that ass."

I didn't laugh.

She poked me. "Lighten up, *mijo*," she said. "We're about to win."

I looked at her and shook my head.

The sidelines were tense as the players lined up for their shoot-out. Julian and the opposing goalie shook hands. Each team chose five players, their best kickers. The roar from the sidelines quieted to an anxious murmur.

Canon City was first. The ref set the ball on the penalty line and the first CC player drilled it straight down the middle. Julian took it in the chest hard, falling to the ground. Ball safe. No goal. Julian jumped up, took a pat on the back from Cate and a cheer from the crowd, and jogged back to the sideline.

Next it was TJ's turn to shoot. Dan Than, our best halfback, trotted out. The opposing goalie stepped into the goal. Than jogged away several paces, lined himself up, took four, and nailed the ball directly at the top left of the goal. CC's goalie dove, reached, and saved it. The opposite crowd cheered.

Five kicks later, both teams were still scoreless. Our team had two kicks left. "Vince!" yelled Coach. "You're up."

"I am so *nerviosa*," said Sonja.

I started paying closer attention to the game. Derek and

Cate or no Derek and Cate, I was beginning to feel like a part of something bigger than myself. I felt like part of an "us," and I wanted us to *win*.

Vince took a few steps back, inhaled, looked at the goal, and launched himself toward the ball. One . . . two . . . three loping steps and he caught the ball with his foot. A deafening *thwack*. He drilled the ball high, strong, and fast . . . and right past the goalie's head and into the net.

Everyone on our side, including me, shouted, "YEAH!" I threw up my hands, jubilant. Sonja reached over for a high five. We connected. Even the fact that it was *Vince* who'd scored the goal suddenly no longer mattered.

The final Canon City player took to the field. Julian took his position. Low, focused, intense, gloved hands out. The ref blew his whistle. The kid raised his hand, sprinted forward two steps, and swung his leg like a mallet at the ball. In a split second, Julian read the kick, dove into the ball's path, threw up his hands, and caught the edge of the ball, nudging it . . .

. . . Right into the top corner of the net.

Our side moaned as the other side exploded into cheers. Julian trotted off the field and into the clutch of players. Coach clapped him on the back. Derek took Julian's shoulders in his hands again. I could make out Julian saying, "I'm sorry."

The score was 1–1. But we still had one more chance to take the lead.

"Griffin!" yelled Coach. "You're on."

Derek patted Julian's shoulders and looked into his eyes. He jogged into position, five steps behind the penalty line. The ref placed the ball carefully on the line.

"It's all you, Griffin!" yelled Vince.

"Let's go, Derek!" yelled Cate from behind the goal line.

The ref blew his whistle. Derek took two slow steps, then three sprinted steps and connected solidly with the ball. *Pow!*

I watched time slow down as the ball traveled through the air, looking like nothing could stop it. Brilliantly, he'd aimed dead center, knowing the goalie would assume he'd aimed for a corner. As the goalie gambled and dove to the left, arms flying, the ball came straight down the middle . . . and right into the middle of the net.

"YEEEEEEEEAAAAAAAAAAAAAAHHHHHHHH!!!!!"

My scream melted into all the other screams coming from our crowd, now over a hundred strong and jumping wildly up and down, bouncing as one. Derek collapsed onto the grass. He was quickly covered by a dozen sweaty soccer players, screaming, "Yeah!!!"

Cate ran out onto the field, sprinting, arm stretched high in a tight fist. She ran to the rapidly growing dog pile of players, hooting, "Woo-hoo!"

Not thinking, I followed along, sprinting out to the heap. Sonja was right behind me.

The players were wildly hugging each other, slapping

each other on the back. Through the bodies I could see Cate, hugging random players, one after the other. Derek was on the other side of the pack, hugging Julian and Vince.

"Go, TJ! Yeaaaaah!" I yelled at the boys, lunging at Derek. I no longer cared about what had or hadn't happened the night before. We were champs!

"Lucas!!" shouted Derek. He leaped out of Julian's grasp and grabbed me, enveloping me in a massive bear hug. "We won! Yeah!"

Julian, jumping up and down, threw his arms around both of us.

From the corner of my eye, I could see Cate struggling to get to where we were. She threw off the arms of the players who surrounded her and pushed through the crowd.

Derek didn't see her coming. He tightened his grip around me. He now had me in a headlock as he high-fived the other players. Screams of, "Griffin! You RULE!" and, "TJ is number one!!!" filled the air.

On her way toward us Cate was intercepted by Vince. He threw his arms around her and slung her over his shirtless shoulders. "Number one! TJ rules!"

Cate gave a "woo-hoo!" before squirming out of Vince's grasp. She grabbed Derek's arm, tearing it from around me and holding it up in the air. He pulled her off the ground. She took his face in her hands and kissed his cheek. He kissed her back, on the mouth.

I stopped cheering and took a step back, stunned. An

instant later, I was sucked into the crowd and away. I squirmed through and walked back to the bench. I now saw the sign. I had to decide whether I was going to read it or not.

"Need a hand?" It was Julian, pointing at the mess of towels and paper cups around the bench. "I can help."

17.

Saturday

I DIDN'T LET JULIAN HELP CLEAN UP. I SENT HIM TO THE LOCKER room with a wave and a "Congratulations." I didn't let Sonja help either. By the time I was done, dusk had fallen and there was no one else out on the soccer fields. I felt a hollow feeling in the pit of my stomach and willed it to go away.

I zipped up the last duffel and walked back to the parking lot. *He couldn't have been with Cate,* I thought. *He was with me.*

By the time I got back to the room to change for the awards ceremony, Derek and Julian had already left. I decided to skip the awards ceremony dinner and take my time showering and getting dressed. I'd miss dinner, but I'd be there for the after party. I wasn't going to miss it like I'd missed the night before. Not a chance.

Too much could happen.

Rrrrrrrrrrrrring! My cell phone went off. The caller ID told me it was Sonja.

"I'm getting dressed," I said. "I'll be there."

"Hurry." She giggled. "Vince is looking cute. Evil Sonja might come out and jump him."

"Gross," I said, hanging up.

I showered, aggressively soaping myself up twice and coaxing the water progressively hotter and hotter. It felt good, and after a while, I felt clean.

I toweled off, brushed my teeth, and went back into the bedroom. I zipped open my duffel to find the jeans and polo shirt I'd planned to wear tonight.

There, poking out of Derek's gym bag, was last night's bottle of Jack Daniels. There was still some left. Should I?

Everyone else at the party would be drunk anyway. So why not? I unscrewed the bottle and poured into a plastic cup, filling it halfway. The rest of the cup I filled with Coke. "To victory," I toasted to my reflection in the window.

I sipped, coughed, sipped, coughed, and sipped again. By the fourth sip, my drink was going down easily. Sonja called again. "We're out in the parking lot!" she said through the laughing in the background.

I hung up and continued to get dressed. I wondered what Derek would be wearing.

By the time I'd finished my drink, I was dressed and ready for the party. I thought about eating a PowerBar since I'd skipped dinner, but decided to have another drink instead. Unfortunately, I'd run out of Coke. So I had to drink the Jack Daniels straight up. It wasn't bad.

Sonja called again. "We're by the pool!"

I poured myself some more Jack as I leafed through the

guest handbook to see where the pool was. "Ah," I said aloud. "It's in the back, past the lobby. Of course."

I felt for my key card as I stepped out of the room. *The pool,* I thought, buzzed. "In the back, past the lobby." I slipped into an empty elevator, pressed ONE, and tried to balance my reflection in the mirrored wall. I kept swaying back and forth and splitting in two. I realized I'd brought along my plastic cup, half full of Jack Daniels. I decided I'd better down it so I didn't get caught with it.

Good thinking, I told myself, throwing it back. I swallowed down a wave of nausea. *Now I won't get caught. So what if Cate hooked up with Derek last night? He came to me afterward. He spooned me. He made me stay.*

I tossed my cup into the plastic trash can by the unmanned check-in desk and headed back down the hallway toward the swimming pool.

As I made it down the hallway, the fuzzy sign came into view. POOL HOURS, 7 A.M.–10 P.M. The letters danced around in my eyes.

Four or five paces away from the door, I heard laughter from the other side. *What if Cate's there? What if they're hooking up again?* I stopped short, suddenly paralyzed. What would I see when I opened that door?

I pictured Cate, sitting on Derek's lap, kissing him between sips of wine as the other players looked on.

I shook the image from my head and forced my feet toward the door. *If they're hooking up again,* I thought, *it's only because I'm not there. He came to me last night after her. He wants me. He is only with her because he is trapped in the closet. And he's begging to be set free.* I knew what I needed to do.

I stumbled through the glass doors and into the outdoor pool area, dizzy. Drunk.

There was a low fence surrounding the pool and about twenty-five lounge chairs arranged haphazardly on the cement deck. A couple dozen bodies were draped over the chairs, and several others were sitting along the edge of the pool. The area was lit mostly by a bright spotlight deep in the pool, which cast a bluish tinge across the deck and across the faces gathered there.

I hazily recognized several TJ soccer players, including Dan Than, who was pacing by the pool, loudly giving his version of the earlier shoot-out to two boys I didn't recognize. I saw Sonja lying back in a lounge chair. Vince was at her feet, arguing with a couple of other players about his goal. There was Julian, lying on a chaise just beyond the towel counter, sipping from a cup and looking up at the sky. At his feet, with her arm draped over his legs, sat Cate. She was dangling her feet in the water.

And next to Cate, kicking his feet in the water too, was Derek.

I leaned in their direction but didn't quite take a step.

"Hey, Lucas!" yelled Sonja.

I threw a half wave.

Derek spun around. "Lucas!" He seemed to be moving too fast, leaving a blur of Derek trails behind him.

He stood up and walked over to me, leaving wet footprints on the deck. "Why weren't you at the dinner?" As he got closer, he came into sharper focus. His eyes were lit, dancing. He'd shaved. He smelled good. But I couldn't rest my eyes on any one spot. I couldn't hold them still. "Want a drink?" he asked, holding out his cup. "Vince brought vodka," he answered. "Here, have a sip. We can share."

I gulped it, drinking deeply. "Yum." I coughed.

"Hey, Lucas!" he spurted. "Think fast!" He jumped behind me, grabbed my arms, and thrust me toward the pool by the shoulders. "Watch out!" He pulled me back. "Saved!"

I gasped and dropped his drink. Derek laughed. "Ha-ha! Just kidding, man," he said. "I wouldn't do that to you, buddy. *I love you, man!*" He said it exaggeratedly, making sure anyone in earshot would hear. *"I love this guy!"* He wrapped his arm around my neck, burying my face in his neck.

The pool disappeared. I stopped thinking. I didn't know where I was or how I got there, but there was Derek. And he loved me. Nothing else mattered.

I took a step back, turning to face Derek head-on. I stood up on my toes and took his face in my hands. I tried to keep my eyes still so I could stare into his. I stared with all my strength, frantically forcing my way into his eyes to see, once and for all, what was there. I would connect. I would find him. I would open the door and let him out.

But he deflected me with a silly grin and that damn sparkle.

If I can't find him in his eyes, I'll find another way. This was the only way I could help him, me, Cate, everyone to face the truth. Enough of all the lies and the games. This was what was right and this was what was fair. It was time.

I stood on my toes, took his face in my hands, and then . . . I kissed him. I pressed my lips to his lips. They were strong, soft, wet, and they gave a little as I pushed against them. I loosened my tongue, letting it graze across his teeth. I felt my spine lengthen and relax as I savored Derek's flavor, warm and alive and savory sweet. I closed my eyes.

Finally, I thought. *Finally.*

I stepped back, eyes still closed, and stumbled a step or two. I swirled my tongue around my mouth. Nothing had ever tasted so wonderful in all of my life. I wanted to remember the taste.

I smiled, opened my eyes, and looked around. What had been a hazy pool scene was now a spectacular tie-dye of colors and movement. I couldn't tell which direction I was facing. Was I standing or sitting?

I looked up at Derek, ready for him to take me by the hand. *Finally,* I thought. *I've saved him.* I found his eyes, ready to collect on the love I knew would be in them.

But there was no love there. Derek looked sick. Woozy. Like he'd just been knocked over the head or kicked in the stomach. He looked dazed.

I screwed up my face, confused. "What?"

His dazed expression grew fearful and angry.

"What the *fuck* are you doing, Lucas?" he yelled, jumping backward and pushing me away like a disease. "What the *fuck*?"

I heard Sonja from behind me. "Oh my God."

18.

Saturday

AND THEN EVERYTHING WENT SILENT, LIKE THE ENTIRE POOL area had been put on mute. I felt eyes on me from every direction, burning, searing, splitting me open. I wanted to run. I wanted out.

And then the silence broke. "You homo!" came the cry. It was Vince, leaping off the lounge chair and lunging at me.

Somehow I ducked his swing, losing my balance and falling to the cement. I caught myself with my arm and forced myself back to my feet, grinning stupidly. I turned toward the door to leave. But one step and there was Vince, arms outstretched, blocking my way. "Where you going, faggot?" He tapped my chest with his fingers, forcing me backward. "Going somewhere?" He pushed me again.

"No," I said, head down.

"I didn't think so," said Vince.

"Vince!" I heard Sonja shout. "Leave him alone. Quit being such a dick!"

"That's what he likes, though," answered Vince. "Dick. Just like you, Sonja. Maybe that's why you're such good friends. 'Cause you both like dick so much!" He turned back to me, raising his hand to push me again. I threw up my hand to block him, knocking back his fists. Vince answered with a growl. "Get away from my dick."

I flinched, stepping backward onto the edge of the pool. My toes curled, gripping the concrete lip.

"Lucas!" I heard Sonja yelling. "Lucas!"

I might have been able to save myself from the fall if I'd pushed back or if I'd tried to balance. But the truth is, at that instant, I didn't see the point. At that instant, I figured I was better off at the bottom of that pool.

So I fell, let myself fall, entered the pool with a painful, slapping splash.

The water was warm, coaxing me to the tile with a gentle thud.

I didn't surface. I didn't want to. I stayed underwater, rolling myself into a ball on the bottom tiles, eyes open. Looking up through the double haze of four feet of water and about fourteen drinks, I watched the room. I saw Sonja screaming at Vince. I saw Vince dragging Derek away from the pool. I saw Sonja turn back to me, eyes wide, staring down at me in the water. But I couldn't hear a thing.

And I saw Cate, standing on the edge of the pool. She looked down at me with an angry glare. She looked over at Derek and Vince, who were beckoning her to join them back inside, then back at me. Sonja pointed down at me, grabbing Cate's arm and yelling.

I wondered how long I'd have to stay underwater before Cate would dive in after me. After all, she'd been a lifeguard.

I knew she'd never leave me at the bottom of a pool, drunk out of my mind. Cate would never let that happen to me. Even though we had gone almost a week "not speaking," we were friends forever. We'd "not spoken" before. But I always knew that Cate loved me. I knew that. And she knew that I loved her.

No, she would never let me drown. So would I let her jump in after me?

Cate turned toward Derek. She turned back toward me. She turned back toward Derek. And then she walked away.

I waited a moment to make sure they'd gone inside, then closed my eyes and surfaced. Only Sonja was there, at the edge of the pool.

"Are you okay?" she asked. "You freaked me out. Here." She held out her arm.

I ignored her arm and hoisted myself out of the pool, suddenly much more sober than I'd been moments ago.

"What is wrong with you, Lucas? What did you just do?" Sonja sounded frantic and exasperated.

I stood, dripping. "Not you too," I said. "Not you too."

"What?" pressed Sonja. "Not me too what?"

"Don't humiliate me, Sonja. Don't lecture me. I'm done." I wrung water from the waist of my shirt.

"You?" she demanded. "Humiliate you? What about what you just did to Derek?"

"Derek?" I breathed, wiping water from my face. "How was Derek humiliated?"

"When you kissed him!" said Sonja, arching her back and tossing her hair over one shoulder. "It was wrong, Lucas. *Loco*. It was so gay."

She said it, and I heard her. I was too gay now even for Sonja. I was getting colder by the second.

Sonja looked at me, shaking her head in pity. "I didn't mean that, Lucas." She walked over to the pool counter. "I'm sorry. I love you. Let's get you some towels."

I didn't know what to believe right then. I didn't know who to trust.

"It's okay, Sonja. You can go join the party. I'll be fine." But even as I said it, I knew it wasn't true.

"Shut up," said Sonja, handing me a towel. "Why did you do it, Lucas? Especially after last night?"

I wiped water off my face. "What happened last night?" I asked. "What do you mean? You wouldn't tell me!"

"Derek didn't tell you?" she asked, reaching up to rub a towel through my hair. "I assumed he would have."

"Tell me *what*?" I demanded.

"That he and Cate hooked up last night," she said. "That's why he was out so late."

"No way," I said. "No way. He was with me."

"Lucas." Sonja shook her head. She didn't have to finish. She didn't believe me.

"He didn't tell me that," I said. "I didn't know." I grabbed another towel and wrapped it around my shoulders.

Suddenly I was totally, wholly exhausted. By all of it.

"Sonja," I said. "Go join the others. I'll be fine."

"No way," she said. "You'll freeze to death."

"It's a pleasant way to go, they say," I answered, sitting down on a lounge chair.

"Not funny," said Sonja sternly.

"Sonja, I'll be okay," I said. "See you tomorrow."

"I'm sorry about what I said," said Sonja. "I don't think you're too gay. I just think you're crazy." Sonja laid a towel over my legs. "Get to bed soon. See you tomorrow for the drive home. Leave around twelve?" She walked out, and I closed my eyes to stop the spinning. For several moments, all I could hear were some crickets in the field beyond the pool.

I opened my eyes. All I saw was stars. The sky was coated in them. I relaxed my gaze and let them all blend together in that hazy mist they make.

"Amazing, huh?" The voice came from the other end of the pool. "So many more here than in Denver."

It was Julian, still on the chaise beyond the towel counter.

"Don't you want to be with the others?" I asked, pulling a towel over my face.

"Nope," he said. "Not really. I'd rather be out here."

I closed my eyes again.

I woke up at sunrise, shivering. I crept back to my room, where I crashed on the couch. Julian was already there, but Derek wasn't.

19.

Sunday

"CATE WENT HOME ON THE BUS," SAID SONJA, SNAPPING HER gum and digging through her purse.

"Good," I said, turning the key in the ignition and watching the fuel gauge rise to half full. "So please say it's just you and me?" I asked wearily.

"Just you and me," said Sonja, lifting her hair out of the way to buckle her seat belt. "And we're *late*. If we're not at the restaurant by four, El Jefe's going to kill us."

"What time is it?" I asked.

"One thirty," she said.

"Then we better hurry!" said Julian, who'd just appeared at the car window, soccer bag draped over his shoulder. "Got room? I missed the bus again."

"Get in," said Sonja, checking her lipstick in the passenger mirror.

We pulled out of the Holiday Inn parking lot and onto the freeway. Within five mile markers, Julian was snoring.

"You were drunk last night," said Sonja.

"I should have eaten dinner."

"Nice try," said Sonja, rolling up her window. "Lucas, what is going on with you this weekend? I'm worried about you, and I'm *never* worried about you. I'm usually only worried about me."

So I told her. I told her about Friday night's party and how it had taken over my room while I'd stayed behind the curtain. I told her about the shots. I told her about Canon City. I told her about staying behind and falling asleep on Derek's bed.

"When I woke up, we were in the same bed," I said.

"So what?" said Sonja. "Lots of players had to share beds. It doesn't mean anything." A state police car whizzed by, giving chase to a speeding BMW SUV. "Nice car," said Sonja.

"Sonja," I said, slowing down to the speed limit. "He was touching me."

"How close?" demanded Sonja. "I'm sure he was just drunk."

"He was spooning me, Sonja," I said, changing lanes to pass an eighteen-wheeler. "I'm not making it up."

I told her about how he'd bolted out of bed this morning and left without saying good-bye. I told her how I'd only seen him on the field yesterday and how he'd never said anything about what had happened. I told her I'd seen how he and Cate were acting together, and how I'd stayed late at the fields to finish clearing up, and how many drinks I thought I'd had before leaving the hotel room last night.

"The rest of the story you already know," I said. "The kiss. The pool. The whole thing."

"Are you *sure* he was spooning you on Friday? It sounds like he was just drunk."

"Yes, he was drunk, Sonja. But I know what I felt. Maybe to you, spooning is nothing. But believe it or not, not everyone gets around as much as you do."

"What are you saying, Lucas?" she snapped. "Are you saying I'm too slutty?"

"No," I said. "No more than you were saying I was too gay last night."

"I'm sorry," said Sonja. "Look, I know how it feels to be embarrassed in public. People are always calling me a slut."

"It's not the same," I said. "You can't know how I feel. You're not gay."

Sonja inhaled slowly. "No, Lucas. I've never been thrown into a pool," she said. "But it's not like I don't know what it's like to be harassed."

"Whatever, Sonja," I said. "I'm alone in this. No one gets it. I have nowhere to go. My friends can't understand me. People at school just think I'm fine all the time. They think they're okay with the gay thing. But calling a guy a *faggot* is the worst thing you can call him."

Sonja didn't answer.

"It's okay, Sonja. I'm used to it. Everything is different for me." I switched lanes to pass a slow-moving camper. "I don't know how anything fits together anymore. I don't belong at TJ. I don't belong at home. I don't know where I belong. I don't know who I'm supposed to be."

"I know what you mean," said Sonja.

"No, you don't," I replied, shaking my head. "You have no idea what it's like."

"Oh, Lucas, give me a break," said Sonja. "You're right, you're the gay one. Waa-waa. Call the waaaambulance, but don't forget, Lucas, I'm a *slut*, remember? It's not like my friends understand what it's like to be called *that* all the time. And it's not like I fit in at home either. Do you think El Jefe is cool with my reputation? Do you think you're the only one who knows what it's like to feel alone? I'm sorry, Lucas. I'm sorry it sucks for you sometimes, but whatever. I have a story too. So do plenty of people."

I clamped my mouth shut. I had no idea what to say. Sonja was sounding like she hated everything as much as I did. She never let it show, but that didn't mean the feelings weren't there.

Maybe Sonja *did* understand.

We sped along the highway in silence, listening to the wind.

We were still about twenty minutes from town when a light flickered on the dashboard, then went dark. Was that the gas light? It hit me that we hadn't filled up with gas since we'd left Denver on Friday. *Crap.*

We'd made it almost to the exit when the car began to sputter and cough. And then stall.

"What's going on?" said Sonja.

"Gas," I said. "We're out of gas."

"So now what?" she asked.

"I don't know," I said. "I guess we walk to a gas station. Or hitchhike."

"Where are we?" she asked.

"What do I look like, Rand McNally?" I answered. "I have no idea."

"Are we near a gas station?" she asked. "What do we do?"

I took out my cell and flipped it open. No service. "It's three forty-five already," I said. "We'll never get there in time."

"We have to get to La Boca," said Sonja. "El Jefe's going to kill us if we're late." She pulled out her phone. "Damn! No service."

Julian surfaced in the backseat, blinking. "What's going on?" he asked.

"Out of gas," I answered. "Does your phone work?"

"Nope," said Julian, looking at his cell.

"Oh, hell."

We sat in the car for a few minutes, bickering about what we should do and who should do it. First I was going to walk up ahead to the nearest exit and get a tow truck to come rescue us. But we didn't know how far that would be. Then Julian was going to walk back to the last exit, which we knew was three miles away, but Sonja said that would take too long. She was starting to panic. "El Jefe . . ."

Finally we decided to hitchhike. I held out my thumb for a few minutes, and while several cars whizzed by, no one stopped. Julian tried, but still, nothing.

"Let me try," said Sonja. She reapplied her lipstick and shook out her hair. Hiking down her jeans and sticking out her butt, she threw up her thumb.

Seconds later, a black BMW SUV came screeching to a halt. The tinted window came rolling down, unleashing the strains of Selena's old hit, "¡*Cobarde*!" "Hi, Sonja!"

It was Alex Norita.

"Hi, Lucas!" he said. "What are you guys doing here?"

"Alex Norita?" said Sonja, mouth hanging open.

"We're on our way home from Pueblo," I said. "We ran out of gas."

"I was just down that way too!" said Alex. "There's a new UFO museum in Trinidad. It's the new Roswell, you know. I went down for the opening party. Do you guys need a lift?"

"How fast can you get us to La Boca?" asked Sonja, climbing into the front seat of Alex's SUV. "Nice car."

We made it to La Boca in record time. Alex and Sonja sang Selena songs in the front seat, and Julian fell asleep on my shoulder in the back.

20.

Sunday

"*FOTOS Y RECUERDOS,*" SANG SONJA, BOPPING THROUGH THE kitchen at La Boca with a tray of salt- and pepper shakers and bottles of hot sauce. El Jefe was barking orders at Sonja's brothers, all focused on their prep work before the dinner rush, still an hour away.

I stood silently behind the wait station, wrapping silverware in bright green polyester napkins.

She just smiled and kept singing, "*Tengo una foto de ti . . .*" as she pushed her way into the dining room. I followed. The restaurant was empty except for table fourteen, where Julian was drooping over a bowl of CCQ and chips, alternating bites with sips from a glass of Coke with lime syrup.

"How's the CCQ, Julian?" asked Sonja, spinning through the room, dropping shakers and hot sauce in the middle of each table.

"Mmmph," answered Julian, mouth full. I wished I were hungry, because it looked good, but all I seemed to be able to stomach today was Diet Coke. I'd been sucking it down like I was in a contest.

El Jefe barged through the swinging door. "Where's Cate?" he barked. He retied his bandanna around his forehead. "Sonja?"

"She'll be here," said Sonja, looking at me and shrugging. "I think." She giggled.

I wrapped another napkin. "I hope not."

"News flash, Lucas," said Sonja, rewrapping a napkin at table four. "Cate is probably coming tonight. It's her job. Even if she doesn't come tonight, you'll see her tomorrow, when everyone at TJ will be talking about it. Are you ready for that?"

I held my hands over my ears. "Can I have a day of denial about that, please?"

"Whatever," said Sonja. "I'm just saying, the sooner you deal, the better." She shook her head.

I didn't answer. The day had been far too long already.

I looked up from my napkin-wrapping and caught a glimpse of myself in one of the mosaic mirrors next to the wait station. I didn't recognize myself. In the bright overhead dining room light, soon to be replaced by supple candlelight for the dinner rush, I looked old, sallow. My eyes were sunken, with dark rings around them, and bloodshot. The pores on the end of my nose were wide open and black. I didn't look like me.

"Can I kill these overhead lights?" I asked Sonja as I looked deeper into the biggest pore. "You could drive a truck through this pore."

I looked over at Julian, who'd turned to the mirror on the wall next to his table. Was he looking at his own pores? Did he even know what a pore was?

"Where's the bathroom?" he yelled.

"Back there," said Sonja, pointing to the HOMBRES sign. Julian leaped up and walked back to the bathroom, his ratty jeans trailing on the floor behind his Birkenstocks.

"We can't turn off the lights until we're done setting up," said Sonja, wrestling with the napkin dispenser on table four. "Speaking of which, Lucas, maybe you could get the candles for the tables? In the kitchen?"

I slipped through the swinging door into the kitchen just as I heard the front door open behind me. Without looking back, I checked the kitchen clock. *Five fifteen,* I thought. *Early birds.* I'd go back out in a minute.

I looked around the kitchen for the candles, not seeing them right away. "El Jefe!" I shouted over the stove. "Where are the candles?"

"*¿Esos?*" he asked, pointing to a tray full of candles on the counter in front of my face.

I smiled, sheepish. "Thanks, El Jefe," I said.

"Wake up!" he barked sweatily, waving his tongs in the air. "*¡Atención!*"

I picked up the tray of candles and turned around just in time to see Sonja crash through the swinging door. She had an aggressive smile. "Wake up, Lucas," she said, wide-eyed. "It's time."

Behind her, standing just beyond the swinging door, was

Cate. I dropped the tray of candles back onto the counter with a crash. I flinched, but El Jefe didn't even look up. I looked at Sonja.

"Cate's here," she said. "And Derek's out front." She stood there in front of me, smiling.

"Derek?" I asked. "What is he doing here?"

"I don't know," she said through her teeth. " Something about missing the bus in Pueblo and riding home with Cate on the Greyhound and getting off at the University of Denver bus station over on University and walking home, only La Boca is on the way. In other words, I don't know why he's here. I don't think even he knows why he's here."

"No." I shook my head fast. "I can't deal."

"Lucas," said Sonja, "Move." She pushed me toward the door, muttering, "Deal. I can't take it."

"Sonja!" I snapped. "Don't—"

She pushed me through the swinging door and into the dining room. There stood Cate in a Cartier-Bresson T-shirt that looked a lot like the one Derek had been in here wearing a couple of weeks ago.

It's probably the same one, I thought bitterly. "Nice shirt," I sneered under my breath. I wouldn't attack Cate out loud. She shouldn't have the satisfaction, and besides, I was too tired. Cate folded her arms across her chest.

"Lucas," said Sonja. "Do you have anything to say to Cate?"

"Not really," I said, not looking at Cate.

"No," said Cate. "I think he's said and done enough already."

I looked at Sonja. "Let the record show that I am the one to blame," I said sarcastically. "Let the record show that I am a bad friend." I fiddled with my apron, which was stuck in a knot. "Story over." I started stomping back toward the kitchen.

"I'm out of here," said Cate. "Come on, Derek."

"Lucas!" shouted Sonja after me. "Grow up!"

"Add that to the record," I said, waving my hand, and I strode into the kitchen. "Immature."

"He's sorry, Cate," said Sonja behind me. "He just doesn't know it yet."

"I am not sorry," I corrected, spinning around and taking a few steps back toward the girls. "I am sick of apologizing. I am sick of being the one who's wrong." I realized now that I was yelling.

"Quiet!" yelled El Jefe, bashing through the swinging door. "¡Callase!"

I sucked in my breath and held it, heart racing, as El Jefe went back into the kitchen. "Hey," I said, regaining my air. "Why did you leave me last night? In the pool?"

"Oh please," she said. "It's not like you were going to drown. There were plenty of people there who could have gotten you out of the bottom of the pool."

"Like who?" I asked. "Who? Sonja?"

"I don't know!" said Cate, flustered now. "But I know you wouldn't have drowned. You know how to swim!" She looked at Derek. "He wasn't about to drown." Derek shifted uneasily and looked at his shoes.

"I was drowning before I even hit the water," I said.

Cate snorted.

"And you walked away. Why did you leave me there, Cate?" I asked.

"What about what you did?"

"I screwed up. I was confused. But I would never, *never* leave you if you'd been knocked down like that. Even if you'd done something wrong. Even if you'd hurt me. I would have picked you up and carried you." I was spitting, foaming, furious. My skin felt hot, like it was sunburned.

Sonja put one arm around my shoulders, another around my waist. "Lucas," she said softly. "Let's sit down."

"No, Sonja," I said, shaking my arm free. "You're the one who wants us to deal with this. So let's deal." I shifted my gaze from Cate to Derek, bearing down on him with my eyes. "Derek," I said. "Did you hook up with Cate on Friday?"

Derek looked at Cate, then looked at me, then back at Cate, not speaking.

"Don't you think I have a right to know?"

"I—" He sat down on the nearest chair.

"Yes, " said Cate. "He and I hooked up on Friday. And last night too. We hooked up! Congratulations! You succeeded."

Congratulations, I thought, grabbing the side of the table for support. I knew I would need it. "Why, Derek?" I leaned on the table and looked down at him. "Why?"

"Why what?" demanded Cate. "Why what, Lucas? What are you talking about?"

I banged my hands on the table, rattling the silverware and sending a red plastic cup flying. "Why?" I seethed at Derek. "Why did you spend the night with me on Friday night after hooking up with Cate?"

"I can't believe this!" shrieked Cate. "What are you even *talking* about? Wake up! Stop lying to yourself!"

Sonja reached for my arm. "That's enough. Come on, come back to the kitchen with me."

I wriggled away from her. "No, Sonja. No. Let's get it all out. If I'm crazy, let Derek tell me I am." I turned to Derek, standing taller. "Derek!" I demanded. "Why did you come to me after you were with Cate?"

"Stop!" yelled Cate. "Stop lying! Stop it!" She threw her hands up over her face.

I stood, holding my position in front of Derek. I knew that all my cards were out now. And for once, I was the one showing them. They could believe me or not. I didn't care. I felt naked but strong.

"He's not lying," came a voice behind us. "Lucas is telling the truth." It was Julian.

Everyone spun to face him. He stood in the hallway just in front of the HOMBRES sign, wiping his hands on his jeans. "What?"

"Julian!" Cate gulped. "Where did you come from?"

"I was taking a whiz. Lucas brought me here for some CCQ. And he's not lying. I saw everything."

"What are you talking about, Julian?" said Cate. I knew that she knew that if it was true, then I wasn't as crazy as everyone thought. If it was true, then it made sense that I had kissed Derek last night.

"Julian," I interrupted. "You don't have to . . ." He was risking Derek's reputation and his own. "It's okay," I said.

"I don't have to what?" he said. "Tell the truth?" He turned to Cate. "Cate, I saw them. And they were spooning. Lucas even tried to get away, but Derek wouldn't let him go. I saw the whole thing." Julian walked over to his table and dunked another chip in his bowl of CCQ.

I tore my eyes away from Julian and planted them on Cate, who was listening hard.

"Julian," she said. "Why would you say that?"

"Why do you think?" he said, dipping another chip. "Because it's the truth."

Cate pinned him with a scrutinizing stare, then turned to Derek.

"Derek," she said. "Is this true? Were you *with* Lucas after you were with me on Friday?"

Derek dropped his head to his knees, collapsing.

"Derek?" she demanded. "Were you with Lucas?"

Derek stood up, looked at me, looked at Cate, then looked back at me. He turned toward the door and with an emphatic push knocked it open and crashed into the parking lot. The door slammed behind him.

Sonja looked at me, flushed. "Okay," she said. "What is going on?" She looked at Cate, then Julian, then me again. "Is he gay or what? Was he with you"—she pointed at

Cate—"or you?" She pointed at me. "What is going *on*?"

I ignored her, turning toward Julian, who'd just changed everything. "Julian," I said. "Why?"

"Because it's the truth," he said, straight into my eyes. "I saw what I saw." He looked at Cate. "I saw what I saw," he said again. "That's all." He dipped another chip in his bowl of CCQ.

"Sonja," I said. "I have to go. Cover for me?"

"No," she said. "You can't just go like that. You can't just walk off. Where are you going?"

"Sonja," I said, taking both of her hands and looking into her eyes. "I love you. But right now I need to be alone. I'll call you, okay?"

"Lucas! You can't just—"

I cut her off. "Sonja." I held up my hand. "Tell El Jefe I owe him one. And you, I owe you one too." I stepped out the door. "I'll call," I said. "Sometime."

I walked out into the parking lot, listening to La Boca's door close behind me. It seemed darker than it should have been at six o'clock. Maybe it was going to rain.

I didn't care.

21.

Sunday

I WALKED SWIFTLY DOWN COLORADO BOULEVARD, NOT LIKE I was late for something, but like I wanted to get away from something. I imagined El Jefe shouting in the kitchen about how I couldn't just leave work like that. I imagined Sonja talking him down, convincing him that they didn't need me on the shift anyway. Cate would stay; Sonja would demand it.

I'd only walked a few minutes when the first drop of rain hit me on the arm. I looked around and realized I was already several blocks away from La Boca. Which direction had Derek walked off in? I didn't even know where he lived. Would I run into him? Would he think I was following him? *Was I* following him?

Hi, he would say.

Why? I would say.

Why what? he would say.

Good-bye, I would say.

Another raindrop hit me, this time on the forehead. I considered turning back but thought, *Who cares if I get wet? Look around. There's no one in sight. Just a few cars, and they don't even see you. No one sees you.*

"No one sees me," I said aloud.

I kept walking, waiting for a third raindrop. I looked back at the sky. "Rain!" I ordered sternly. "Rain already! Jesus! What are you waiting for?"

I hit the corner of Colorado Boulevard and Iliff Street and made a left, toward Observatory Park. I was still a good hour's walk from home, but I didn't care.

How had I lost track of myself so completely these weeks? How had I coiled myself into this corner?

I needed a friend, a best friend, but I couldn't even call her because I'd so completely wrecked our friendship. I felt like poison.

Out of the left corner of my eye, I noticed a figure walking up Steele Street just as I approached the park, but I decided to ignore it.

The grass was damp. The water began soaking through my sneakers.

I reached the park just as the thunder let loose overhead with a deafening crash. The thick raindrops started falling faster, dropping heavily from the sky with thuds on the grass. I sat down, drenched.

"Lucas," came a voice from behind me. I flinched, gasped, and spun around. It was Julian. Raindrops were beading on his crew cut and falling onto his nose, cheekbones, lips. He wiped his hand across his eyes, staring at me. "There's a reason," he said.

I looked at him standing there, just as wet as I was. "What did you say?"

"There's a reason, Lucas," he said again. "A reason I said what I said. A reason besides the truth."

"Julian," I said, "I don't know what you're talking about." I lay down in the wet grass.

He lay down next to me.

"You'll get wet," I said. "Cate won't like it."

"Who cares?" he replied, wiping his eyes again. "Lucas, I didn't have to tell the truth. You know that."

"Thanks," I said. "I appreciate what you did. My life is a pile of crap anyway, but thanks."

"Lucas," he said. "There's another reason."

"What are you talking about?" I asked.

And then Julian, shy, sleepy Julian, leaned over and kissed me.

I lay there motionless, feeling the water squishing into my clothes. I sat up and rubbed my eyes.

He stood up, dropped his hands into his pockets, and backed away. "I guess I'll see you later."

I sat there in the wet grass, amazed and suddenly exhausted. I watched him walk into the storm.

22.

Sunday

I WAS STILL TOTALLY SOAKED THROUGH WHEN I FINALLY MADE IT home. I didn't care. Mom wasn't home when I got there.

I shed my clothes and stood in the hottest shower I'd ever had in my entire life. Then I climbed into bed.

I'd never been so tired. And not even that kind of tired where you can just drop your head to the pillow and let it all go, crying yourself to sleep. I was that kind of tired where you lie there unable to *do anything*.

I felt used up. I wished I could trade myself in for a new me, a fresh me.

Maybe even a straight me. I mean, wouldn't it just be easier to be straight? Then at least I'd have a track to follow. Date, get married, have a couple of kids, call it a life.

Sure sounded nice.

I wanted to cry. I really did. I thought if I could cry, then maybe I'd finally fall asleep. People were constantly doing that in songs, crying themselves to sleep. Why shouldn't I?

And besides, if I could fall asleep, I could count on those few precious moments tomorrow morning, on the walk from my bed to my toothbrush, where I wouldn't yet remember what'd happened this weekend. For those moments, everything would be fine. It'd just be another day and I'd just be brushing my teeth.

But to get there, to have those moments of forgetfulness, I'd have to fall asleep first.

I was too scared to sleep. I knew that if I lay in the dark, silent but awake, with my mind too tired to think, then I would somehow be safe. At least I'd know where I was and what I had to fear. But as soon as I slept, there was no telling where my mind would go. I thought about calling Cate, but I didn't know what I'd say. I wasn't sure if I was more mad or sorry. I was dreading Monday.

I lay for minutes, or hours, or days, before sleep took over. Deep, dark, dead sleep. The kind where you don't even turn over and you're not even sure that you breathed all night.

By the time I woke up, Monday had already come and gone. I'd slept through school, and I was starving. The clock said seven forty, so I flipped on a *CSI* that I'd TiVo-ed and poured out a bowl of Frosted Flakes. I folded myself into the couch and started in on the sweet, sugary, crunchy flakes, swimming in whole milk.

I was crunching away when Mom came through the front door.

"You're alive!" she said. "That's good." She gripped my

shoulders and kissed the back of my head. "You were still here when I left for work this morning. I tried to wake you up, but you were so exhausted, I just let you sleep."

I didn't know what to say, so I shoved another spoonful into my mouth. I chewed and swallowed. "What time is your date tonight?" I asked. I wanted her out of the house so I could mope around some more.

She tossed her purse on the couch and kicked off her pumps. "I canceled," she said, "so we could have dinner together."

I stopped chewing and looked at her, suspicious.

"Okay, I lied. I got canceled *on*," she said, grabbing a bowl from the cupboard and pouring out some flakes for herself. She turned and I saw a flash of concern in her eyes. "Hey, you doing okay?" I nodded quickly and unconvincingly. "If you want to talk about anything, you know you can always . . ." But she left it at that and she didn't persist. And I was grateful for that.

We finished our bowls watching *CSI* together.

"I love you, honey," she said during a commercial. I didn't answer out loud, but in my head I thought, *I love you, Mom.*

I went to bed that night without even checking my messages.

23.

Tuesday

TUESDAY MORNING WAS JUST LIKE ANY OTHER MORNING, ONLY I knew I'd be entering school with the gossip of the year hanging over my head. There was no way it hadn't been topic A in the TJ halls yesterday. I wondered how Cate had dealt with it. Or Derek. Or Sonja. She'd left me like nine messages yesterday, which I hadn't listened to until this morning.

"Lucas, I am an asshole. I'm so sorry," said Cate, standing beside my locker with Sonja. "I don't know what else I can say. I don't know what happened." The ever-present din of the student body held court behind her, ebbing and flowing and schooling and dropping and devouring itself up like sea life.

I wasn't sure I was ready for her apology. I didn't know how to respond. I shut my locker and spun the dial, wondering how Sunday night had played out for her. Had she hooked up with Derek again?

"Did you hear her?" asked Sonja, hand on hip, staring me down with a hair flip.

"Don't worry about it, Cate," I said. I smiled weakly and started off toward calc. "It's no big deal." I pushed into the crowd.

Cate trotted after me, breathing at my heels. "Lucas, wait up."

"*¡Mijo!*" snapped Sonja. "Wait!" She scuffled in step behind Cate.

Instead of slowing my stride or moving to the side of the hallway, I aimed for the center.

"We didn't know," said Cate.

"Whatever," I said. "What you mean is, you didn't believe me."

Cate grabbed my arm and forced me to stop in the middle of the hallway, swarming with freshmen. "We believe you now."

"Fag!" yelped Vince, brushing by.

"Shut up, Vince," said a random voice in the crowd. I couldn't tell who'd said it. Someone else hissed.

"Eat me, Vince," said Sonja, holding up her hand.

"Ooh," said Vince. "Gladly." He started walking away.

"Fuck off," I said, loud and clear. "Go to hell, Vince."

"What?" He spun around. "What did you say, Lucas?" He stepped toward me, arms outstretched.

"I said, 'Go to hell,'" I repeated. I wasn't scared of Vince anymore. Too much had happened already.

"And fuck off," said Cate. "Don't forget fuck off." She stood tall next to me.

"So that'd be a 'go to hell' and a 'fuck off,'" said a voice behind me, which I knew was Derek's. "In whichever order you choose."

I turned to see Derek, looking not at Vince, but at me. "What's up, Lucas?" he said casually.

I swallowed hard and shrugged. "Nothing," I said. "Nothing."

Derek looked at me, then at Cate, then back at me. "Later," he said, smiling weakly.

"'Bye, Derek," said Sonja gesturing toward the other end of the hall. "Weren't you on your way somewhere else?"

Derek opened his mouth to speak, then clamped it shut. He walked away. I watched him and wondered if he had any idea.

"See?" said Cate. "Everything is back to normal. We're back at school, we're all together, we have calc in two minutes, Vince is still being an asshole. And no one really seems to care about what happened in Pueblo."

I raised one eyebrow.

"Yesterday afternoon that freshman kid Aaron Welles got caught taking a little after-school 'swim lesson' with Ms. Eisley, the hot new girls' swim coach," Sonja said, by way of explanation. "*Way* more interesting than that stuff at Pueblo."

"It's always something, isn't it?" I shook my head.

"So now everything is okay," Cate said. "Or close enough."

"I don't know," I said. And I didn't. I didn't know what I felt, what I wanted, what I thought would happen next. I knew I'd hurt Cate and I was truly sorry for that. I knew I needed to apologize, only I didn't know how.

"Don't be like that, Lucas!" yelled Sonja. "We are making an effort here. Step up!" She threw her hair off her face. "Look at me!"

"I am sorry," said Cate sticking her head up over Sonja's shoulder. "For not believing you. I am sorry for not choosing you when you needed me at the bottom of that pool. I was wrong. I got crazy."

"Yes," I said. "You did."

"Look," said Sonja impatiently. "She wasn't the only one who got crazy, *mijo*. Do you accept her apology or not? We don't have all day."

"It's not that easy." I knew I'd messed up—I'd been a bad friend and selfish. Why was it so hard to admit that?

"Uh, yeah," said Sonja. "It actually *is* that easy. She apologizes, you accept. Then you apologize, and you do it backwards. It's like an apology sixty-nine."

I snickered. I couldn't help it. Things were different, but not *that* different.

"I'm sorry, Lucas," said Cate, moving in front of Sonja.

"Things got real bad, real fast," I said.

"You weren't exactly a saint, Lucas," she said. "You played me too."

"I know," I said. "I guess I lost myself." I stood back,

looking my girls up and down. I guessed I needed them. "I'm sorry," I said. Cate and I hugged, right there in the hallway. We held each other tightly. It was good to have her back.

"I hate boys," I said.

"No, you don't," said Cate.

"No, I don't," I replied.

"I'm gonna cry," Sonja sniffled.

I pulled back from the hug. "Listen, you guys, I have an announcement to make. I am officially out of the matchmaking business. You bitches are on your own from here on."

Alex Norita swept by, head bobbing, white iPod earphone wire slicing across his black mock turtleneck. "Hi, Sonja," he said. "*¡Bidi-bidi bom-bom!*"

Sonja reached out and yanked his phones, which came tearing out of his ears. "Are you listening to Selena?" she said.

"*La reina,*" said Alex. "*¡La reina!*" He grabbed her waist and started swiveling his hips wildly. "It's called the washing machine," he said. "*La máqina.*" And then he walked away.

"Oh my God," said Sonja.

"What, you can't believe he knows the washing machine?"

"No," she said. "I can't believe he's *good* at it."

"Although," I said, "I *could* make an exception. Hey, Alex!"

We walked for a while, not rushing to calc.

"How's Julian?" I asked Cate.

Cate and Sonja looked at each other and smiled.

"I was wondering when you were going to ask about him," said Cate. "He told us everything."

"What do you mean?" I cocked my head back. "Everything *what*?"

"Everything," said Sonja. "I was shocked." She bugged her eyes out in mock surprise. "Shocked."

"You knew?" I said.

"Lucas," said Sonja, "the kid has been crushing on you for the longest time. You and Cate are the only two who couldn't see it."

Suddenly I felt guilty that Julian had seen Derek and me together.

"Did you have any idea," I asked Cate, "that your perfect baby brother was gay?"

"Nope," she said. "Not a clue. But it only makes me love him even more. He's even more perfect. Because now I know how brave he is." She smiled at me. "And I know how brave *you* are."

"Well," I said. "I'm glad he's going to deal with it."

"He also said he's hot for you," said Sonja. "Well, not exactly in those words, but you know what I mean."

"He did?" I asked, anxious. "Oh no." I turned to shake my head at Cate. "I can't go out with him. He's your brother."

"So?" she said. I was surprised.

"So, that would be like you dating my mother!"

"Ooh, hot," said Sonja, nudging Cate. "And she's at her sexual peak!"

"Okay, stop there," I said. "I'm sorry I brought that up."

"So," said Cate. "What do you think about Julian? He's pretty cute, huh?"

"No," I said.

"No?" challenged Cate.

"I mean, yes, he's cute. But no, I can't date him." The bell rang.

"Why not?"

I opened my mouth to post a witty comeback, but there wasn't one. The truth was, Julian *was* cute. And he was honest and brave and admirable. Which was more than I could say for Derek. I started walking more quickly toward calc, hoping for a quick escape.

"Lucas," said Sonja. "Slow down. Can you work with us?"

"I told you, Mindy Matchmaker," I said. "I am done with boys!"

"Oh, please," said Sonja. "We've heard that before."

"Besides," said Cate. "We're not talking about boys. We're talking about Julian. So, you free Sunday afternoon? Because I heard he wants to see the new Jackie Chan movie. Can you make it?"

"Jackie Chan?" I said as we approached the door to calc. I looked at her, then at Sonja. "When will this madness end?" I asked.

"Never, *mijo*," said Sonja, kissing my cheek. "If we're lucky."

24.

Sunday

SO I MET JULIAN AT THE CINEPLEX AT THREE O'CLOCK. I WAS nervous, I think. I'm not sure. It wasn't the same kind of nervous I'd gotten when I was around Derek. That was a loud, throbbing nervousness, a flow of electricity from my stomach through my limbs. This nervous was more like the not-knowing-what-to-expect kind of nervous. The what-have-I-gotten-myself-into kind of nervous.

I wondered if Julian would be different. Would he all of a sudden start opening doors for me, holding my hand, buying me popcorn?

"Hey," he said when I met him under the marquee. He was in ratty jeans and Birks, scratching his crew cut. I saw a dimple in his cheek when he smiled. I'd never noticed that before.

"Hey," I said, smiling back and running my hands through my hair. Sonja had offered to help me get dressed, but I'd just thrown on the same old green-and-yellow Adidas and a pair of jeans.

He didn't hold the door open for me when we went in, and he didn't buy me popcorn. But the movie was good and it was easy being with Julian. We laughed at the same jokes and cheered at the same fights. But we didn't touch knees. We didn't share a Coke. I couldn't feel the pull I'd felt with Marcus or Derek. There was affection there, a tenderness for Julian. I owed him a lot. I owed him my friends. And the way he'd showed himself to me on Sunday night kind of made me love him.

But I wasn't desperate to find a way inside Julian.

After the movie, it was time for me to go to work. "Can I ride with you?" asked Julian. "Maybe have some CCQ before I head home? I can take Cate's car."

"Sure thing, Jackie Chan," I said, unlocking the doors of the Subaru. "And thanks for the movie. That was cool."

We sped up Colorado Boulevard toward Evans and La Boca, recounting the best fight scenes in the movie.

"About the other night," he said as we pulled into the parking lot of La Boca. "Sorry if I freaked you out at the park."

I wasn't sure what to say. "I was being pretty freaky myself that night," was what I came up with. It seemed to fit.

"There weren't any stars out that night," said Julian. "In that rain."

"I didn't notice," I said. "But I guess you're right."

He looked over at me and smiled. I smiled back. "Friends?" I asked.

"Friends," he said.

We walked into La Boca, where Sonja was doing the washing machine with Cate in a dining room full of empty tables. They didn't see us walk in; they just kept dancing. *"Bidi-bidi bom-bom . . ."* sang Sonja. "Move your hips, Cate! Like this!" Sonja's peasant top was falling off her shoulder, her hair flying around it. She spun and knocked over the tray of salt- and pepper shakers that sat on the table behind her. *"¡Ay!"* she yelled as they all crashed to the tile floor.

"¿Qué paso?" yelled El Jefe from the kitchen. *"¡Callate!"*

"Hey," I said, letting the front door slam behind us.

"Lucas!" yelled Sonja.

"Julian!" yelled Cate.

Julian and I looked at each other and smiled. He went to sit down at table eleven, where Cate jumped into his lap. "So? What happened?"

I went to grab an apron from the wait station. "CCQ!" I yelled through the swinging door.

I turned and walked over to Sonja, who was bent over picking up salt- and pepper shakers. "Yeah, what happened?" she asked. *"¡Digame!"*

"The movie was good, don't you think, Julian?" I crouched down to help.

"Yeah," he said, smiling at me. "Not bad. But I doubt there'll be a sequel."

He and I laughed. Cate and Sonja looked at us like we were crazy. Selena started singing *"Amor prohibido . . ."*

Just then my cellie started to vibrate in my pocket. I checked the caller ID: ALEX NORITA.

"Hey, Sonja!" I said, handing her the phone. "I think it's for you."